MW01275302

Presently Untitled

Sara De Armon

PublishAmerica
Baltimore

ISBN: 1-4137-2470-1
PUBLISHED BY
PUBLISHAMERICA, LLLP.
www.publishamerica.com
Baltimore

Printed in the United States of America

I would like to dedicate this book to my parents, my family, and my friends; Stacy and Nancy. May we all fight the Matthews of the world together.

Chapter One

FOR WEEKS THE KENNINGSTONS had been planning their trip to the South of France. The housemaids and butlers had been hastily packing and unpacking, at Mr. and Mrs. Kenningstons' strict request, nothing but the finest of clothing and toiletries. The house was simply buzzing with anticipation for their trip to the sunny beaches that awaited them.

"Do remember to pack your swimwear this year, darling. I so dread searching for proper attire at the Cannes shops, their styles are usually a bit modern for a man of your...um, current stature." Mrs. Kenningston has always been strong-minded and never afraid to speak her mind when it came to her husband's shortcomings.

Married for nearly eighteen years, Mr. Kenningston had grown quite accustomed to his dear wife's openness and, in fact, had become pleased to see that his only child, Katherine, had bestowed some of these very same qualities. "Yes, dear. I am aware of that and I sincerely thank you for your keen interest in my personal appearance." Mr. Kenningston winked sarcastically to his wife.

It was a summer tradition for the Kenningstons to travel each year with two members of their parish, and closest friends, Mr. and Mrs. Wells. But it was this particular year that Katherine decided to stay behind to endeavor herself in her studies. Being a blossoming lady of particularly fine upbringing and wealth, she also felt it necessary to spend her summer preparing for her coming-out ball in the autumn. Though she felt that this was somewhat archaic, this was a time-honored tradition of the elite class of local young women coming of age. Secretly, Katherine had also decided that this would be a nice excuse to have the run of the house while her parents were away, to sleep late and do what ever else she pleased. This included possibly inviting a few close friends to manor, something that her parents forbid her to do without them present. As modern as the Kenningstons were, they still wanted to raise their daughter with the esteem and etiquette that the local socialites expected, and having a house full of young women sipping the cellar wines at all hours of the night was hardly the acceptable thing to do.

The Kenningston family was recognized as one of the wealthiest families in the county which presented a somewhat secluded upbringing for the young Katherine. The Kenningston name had been known to represent wealth and status for many generations and their distant relatives had been known to have once been of high ranking in Parliament. The grand manor that they lived in was admired and envied by almost everyone who entered it. With lavishly tall stone walls and ornate entrances, fountains, and pools, it was an elaborate display of luxury and had brought nothing but a sense of comfort to those who entered it. There was a large pasture for the many horses that the family owned and gardens designed to the family's liking with roses, heather and boldly scented lavender.

Katherine, though an only child, was never alone. She had

staff to accommodate her every need, including Ashton, who seemed to thoroughly enjoy caring for the girl. He had a kind and gentle nature that appealed to everyone who met the man. Although his manner was often very quiet, Ashton had a way of making everyone feel comfortable and at ease. He was known for his work to tirelessly meet the family's needs, coordinating the staff and servants, allowing the house to run smoothly.

"With the uprising of the local townsfolk, do you really think it safe to leave your young daughter behind to care for the manor? I mean they have done many a cruel thing to excuse themselves from paying the land tax that they are indebted to us for," Lady Wells stated.

"Oh please, dear woman, whatever would you do if you hadn't anything to worry about. Ashton has been a servant of theirs for years and I am sure that he is quite capable of assisting the run of the household while they are away. After all…he does it every summer." Mr. Wells lit his pipe. "He is a finely educated man and has a lot to offer the young Katherine. His father, God rest his soul, was also a well-cultured man so I do not worry about him being in charge of dear Katherine." Mr. Wells then scoffed loudly. "Besides, they haven't been able to positively link the attacks to the tax situation. That is purely speculation at this point. Mr. Ashton will surely be more than enough security. Just look at the sheer size of that man. You would think that he was one of the Queen's own guards!"

"Yes, Mrs. Jane, Ashton has proven himself time and time again to be a loyal manservant, beyond the call of duty, and I have nothing but the utmost respect for him. I am most certain that he will care for our dear Katie, just as he always has." Mr. Kenningston followed suit and lit his cigar eloquently, inhaling deeply then spoke. "He practically never leaves her side, and I feel confident that he would protect her at all costs, no matter how tragic the event." Ashton, being his most valued employee, had also grown to be practically part of the

Kenningston family, attending all functions and everyday life events openly.

"I hope that I haven't offended you, John… It's just that I don't know if I would be comfortable leaving a young girl such as Katherine for a whole summer, without so much as a proper governess. After all, Mr. Ashton still draws her bath!" Mrs. Jane put her white satin-gloved hands to her face to appear dramatic.

Mr. Wells just shook his head at the distasteful comment knowing his dear wife always knew the precise way of humiliating him in front of other people.

"Jane," Mrs. Kenningston calmly interjected. "Mr. Ashton has been with our Katie since she had barely turned eight, I dare not think that you are accusing him of any improprieties. He will care for our dearest Katie as he has so many summers in the past…baths and all. I refuse to hear any more of acquiring a governess while we are away on holiday. This will probably be our Katie's last summer at home before she will marry a befitted suitor; therefore, it is important to us to let her enjoy her last season of her childhood. If the dear girl wants to stay at home with her books and lessons…so be it. This is the end of this conversation, Mrs. Jane." Mrs. Kenningston rose, made a quick curtsy, and gracefully exited the room. She had a strong will about her that often, quickly but tastefully, put people in their place when needed.

"Please forgive my dear lady, she always gets a tad over excitable just before our journey, as you know. We mustn't pay any attention to her. She just needs that extra bit of control when it comes to conversation. She just would not be herself if she did not have the run of things. Come now, we must have tea before the coaches arrive to collect the steamers." Mr. Kenningston then turned to the hall where Ashton had just been seen and quickly called out to him. "Ashton, we are now ready for tea!"

Ashton returned within minutes carrying a caddy of tea and crisp linen napkins. He always had a way of anticipating the needs of the master and lady of the house which is what made him such a priceless treasure to the family. The large-built, formally dressed servant always made an extra effort to please the Kenningstons whenever possible. It was their generosity after all that cared for his aging father until he passed some many years ago. Ashton took his father's place as their lead manservant as it was tradition to do so. He felt obligated to continue on with his father's work, caring for the Kenningston family, as they had once cared for his. It had become his passion to care for the family and their young daughter for the past nine years. He had become so close to the family that he soon became Miss Katherine's personal hand and usually assisted her with her tasks of the day, right down to choosing and preparing the miss's dresses and garments for her. Katherine had grown so accustomed to Mr. Ashton being in her presence, despite her ingrained modesty, she thought nothing of having him assist in her bathing, dressing, and combing her long auburn tresses. He had slowly become a necessary part of Katherine's pampered everyday life.

It was he, who in fact, being so many years her senior and so very wise with age, explained to Miss Katherine the woes of womanhood when she was a mere thirteen. She had awoken early that morning to find her bedclothes messed and screamed with terror for fear of bleeding to death. He quickly calmed her with his words on this very delicate manner, assisting her with her sheets. He normally would have beckoned Mrs. Kenningston to intervene with this matter, but she was once again away visiting relatives and the entire lady staff were in town acquiring sundries. Katherine had soon begun to trust Ashton and often spoke with him about matters that she would feel uncomfortable asking her parents or even her pastor.

Their relationship, although always proper, had grown to form a bond like no other. He was always in attendance of her studies, standing militant in the shadows, awaiting Miss Katherine's call. It was because of his very presence, that she had matured to be such a secure, though oftentimes, stubborn, young lady. Ashton had lately found that Katherine had become quiet possibly a little too self-assured and sometimes downright obstinate.

Mr. and Mrs. Kenningston were grateful for the work and efforts that Ashton did for them and trusted him as if he were a part of the Kenningston family. The couple thought nothing of leaving their dear Katherine in the charge of Ashton, sometimes for weeks at a time. They were often overheard telling their friends and church members about how wonderful Ashton's talents were in caring for the manor. Almost instantly they had become completely at ease with Ashton around. Katherine often chose the companionship of her attendee rather than her parents and their boring talk of politics and finances.

Chapter Two

IT WAS A BRIGHT, airy day when the Kenningstons and the Wellses left for the upper-class district of the coast of France. Katherine had followed the Kenningstons' coach for nearly a mile riding bareback on her fancy stallion, much to Mrs. Wells's despair, with Mr. Ashton following close behind watchfully. "Farewell, Mum! I shall see you shortly. Have a safe voyage!" Her expensive combs dangling hopelessly and the ends of her dark auburn locks. Miss Katherine had never much cared for looking fancy, and, in fact, dreaded the coming season when she would have to be bound up in the latest finery, trying to impress some astute gentleman, simply so that he may give her that disgusting animal-like look at her bosom when her parents weren't looking. The very thought appalled her. She was quite content at the manor where she may run about as she pleased with no one but dear Ashton to keep her in check.

Shortly after dusk Katherine finished her first supper alone in the grand house. Ashton had served her pork ribs and red sauce, which her parents felt were impolite for people of proper foundation to consume, and she ate to her content. The other staff sat in the kitchen giggling secretly to themselves, happy to see Miss Kenningston enjoying her newfound freedom.

"Ashton, won't you join me for a little supper?" Katherine felt a bit uncomfortable eating alone and was desperate for some conversation.

"No, thank you, miss. I have already eaten." He handed her a fresh napkin motioning for her to wipe the spot of sauce on her chin.

Katherine smiled childishly at her servant. She always welcomed his presence, though he was a man of few words. "Mr. Ashton, what do you think that we should do these next few months? Maybe I will take up that embroidery that you are always hounding me with." She winked at him teasingly.

"The day you take up embroidery instead of trumping around on that horse of yours is the day that I will promise to do just the opposite." Ashton chuckled. He knew that though his own horsemanship was quiet adequate, it had never been one of his greatest talents. Katherine had been trained by the finest horse masters in England and always shown a great interest in the sport.

After her solemn supper, she went to her exquisite rock-lined garden pool for a swim, as she did every night much to her parents' opposition. The summers at the manor always seemed to be filled with warm nights and crickets chirping somewhere in the great distance. The large house had many stone pathways that led through the richly manicured gardens to the open pool area. She stood on the southernmost bank with the water lilies glittering in the moonlight, and quickly removed her dresses and bustle. Ashton assisted her out of her girdle and underclothes and she swam like a child in the tepid dark water. Katherine had been swimming in this pool nearly every summer night since she was a small child. As she quietly floated on the glassy surface of the water, the stars above her seemed to be strangely brighter on this night than she had ever remembered. It was as though they were telling her that from this night on, things were going to be different. This was going to be the summer that she would always remember.

The pool was routinely her favorite place to relax and enjoy some quiet contemplation with her servant Ashton. She would spend every evening in this pool during the warmer months, enjoying its stillness and calming effect that it had on her. Ashton did not protest because of her deep fondness of this place and many memories involved with it. She had once dived in the icy pond one New Year's Eve as a retort to the taunting neighborhood boys who had said that no girl would do such a thing and survive. If it weren't for Ashton watching her every move, expecting the worst as he always had, she might have drowned in that very pool. After retrieving her still body from the water, he safely carried her limp and hypothermic to the servant's quarters which were the closest. He then carefully placed her in a warm bath, slowly replacing the life that had nearly drawn out of her. He never spoke a word of this to the Kenningstons, knowing that Katherine would be reprimanded severely. This act of kindness seemed to strengthen their friendship and trust for each other beyond what either had expected.

Her parents were now gone for the summer and she was going to enjoy every last minute of their absence. She gaily swam in the pool in the cool white light of the moon, contemplating the year to come. "Ashton, I fear that this is my last summer at the house and I really don't want to leave. I know that after the ball in September I am supposed to find a proper suitor and am expected to enjoy him pawing all over me much like cousin Thomas in a cake shop, but the thought of all of this repulses me." She pretended to shudder. She paused a moment before speaking again. "What do you think I should do? I cannot possibly spend the rest of my life with some boy, playing house, spewing babies out of my...well, you know where. The thought positively disgusts me." She made a spitting sound as she dunked under the water. The moon made full acknowledgement that her thin body had completely blossomed into womanhood. She swam without the slightest bit of embarrassment.

Mr. Ashton replied with his eyes straight ahead, as he always did, in that formal fashion that was always his demeanor. "Yes, Miss Katherine, but it is of every lady's future to be betrothed of a suitor that is decided for that lady. You have spent many years preparing for such an occasion. And with the latest uprising in the townspeople, it is of the utmost importance for you to choose a man with some knowledge of politics. Love will come later and soon you will learn to enjoy all the aspects of a proper marriage." Ashton realized that he had spoken out of turn and quickly apologized for his outspokenness but was relieved that she was showing at least some interest in the subject.

Katherine laughed at him as she often did when he reminded her of her parents. "OK, Ashton, you win, I will try to do as I am told. But let me inform you now, that I will never be happy as a manor wife. I am positively terrified at the prospect of having children. Besides, I am quite satisfied living here with Father and Mum. Not to mention that I couldn't possibly imagine life without you hovering about constantly." She flashed him a witty smile. Katherine swam bosom exposed, light reflecting off her every curve. She was not the slightest ashamed when Ashton was present, and in fact, hadn't really noticed that she had become an astonishing beautiful woman far beyond her years.

"No, ma'am, I don't suppose that you will," Ashton stated quietly. He knew that in a few short months time, possibly even a year, she would be dealing with all of the tragedies of marriage. She would soon be used and tossed aside and ignored when she was no longer wanted, as this was an acceptable practice with the local gentlemen. The Kenningston family was widely known for their large estate and assets and Ashton knew that the Lady Katherine would have no trouble finding a gentleman that would want to become a part of this entitlement. Not to mention Katherine's unique beauty that would surely gain many of the gentlemen's attentions.

"I feel that there is just way too much emphasis in this whole marriage thing and that you men need to just leave us women well enough alone." She splashed Ashton square in the face and quickly swam away laughing to avoid a scolding.

"If that were possible, I most assure you that we would." He wiped his face with the handkerchief that he pulled from his breast pocket. "I guarantee it."

After an hour, Ashton helped Katherine dry herself and dress into her night robe before retreating back to the house. He tucked her into bed and bid her good night before returning downstairs to finish his remaining chores.

Chapter Three

THE NEXT FEW WEEKS were as they always were; Katherine dawdling about the house as she always did, brushing up on her music lessons. Ashton accompanied her a few times into town only to have her promptly return due to the unstableness of the townspeople. The head of the county had raised the tax due from the property renters and these very renters thought that this was an elaborate scheme from the owners to extract more money from them. Two deaths had been reported to be possibly related to this matter. Because of the town's recent state of alarm, it was only logical to confine Miss Katherine to the manor. Her father was one of the wealthiest landowners this side of town and therefore his household could possibly be targeted by the angry commoners.

Katherine had spent the passing days in the garden, pruning the roses that were ordered from the gardens of London and dining in the servant's dining room, though it was restricted from her at her parents' request. He parents were determined to raise their only daughter with all the manners and etiquette that a lady should bestow. Ashton decided that despite his master's request to keep Miss Katherine in the utmost of class, it would be beneficial for her to enjoy spending the summer as she saw fit, within respectful limits. He did, however, assist Katherine in preparing for a gala for her closest friends, which was unfortunately thwarted by protesters who had blocked the road to the manor in efforts to make their opinion on the current tax status known. Nevertheless, Katherine invited all of the servants, stablemen, and butlers to the gala in their stead and it was magnificent. This was an extravagant event of caviar, champagne, and even ice cream flambé. Though completely prepared by the house servants themselves, it was enjoyed nonetheless. They all sang, danced, and filled themselves with these delicacies, chatting until the sun lightened the dawn sky. Even Ashton seemed to be in unusually festive spirits.

One summer morning, Ashton began to clearly see Katherine was once again beginning to feel lonely in the grand manor with no one to socialize with but the servants, so Ashton decided to arrange a surprise party for Katherine. Since the party she had planned weeks before had not turned out as planned, he knew that she would be in need of some sort of contact with the outside world, just to keep her spirits high. He had sent the invitations to Katherine's friends' parents requesting permission to have their attendance by post to maintain discretion; three of the girls had replied stating that they would be honored to attend.

After giving the servants special instructions for the get-together, Ashton announced to Katherine that he would be going into town for supplies. "Excuse me, Miss Katherine, I will be going into town for a few hours. I am going to take the stable boys with me as an escort, just in case we run into any trouble."

Katherine peered over the top of her book uninterestedly. "See you when you get back."

Three hours later, Katherine heard the coach slowly return. She remained seated, trying intently to remain interested in her dull novel. Half of an hour later, Katherine heard Ashton call her to the dining room for lunch. She rose slowly, deciding that she was famished, looking forward to filling her stomach with one of Ashton's latest culinary creations.

Katherine entered the dining room and instantly was instantly flabbergasted. "Surprise!" There standing before her were three of her dearest friends from her childhood and church.

"Teresa? Chloe? Rosemary? What on earth are you doing here?" Instantly they all embraced, jumping up and down hysterically. "My dears, why are you here?" Katherine had tears in her eyes. She hadn't been forced to attend church since her parents had left, so she hadn't seen much of the outside world these past few weeks.

"Mr. Ashton wrote to our mums and asked if we could come. I had to beg and beg, but she finally allowed me to go. We get to sleep over tonight!" Teresa was beaming.

"Oh, Ashton! Thank you!" Katherine laughed. Her eyes then roved to the fanciful painted teacups and dishes set before her. "A tea party! Ashton, what on earth put you up to this?" Katherine seated herself as the other girls had done.

"Just thought that you needed some company. I must leave you for a moment while I take the ladies' things to the spare rooms that I have prepared for them." Ashton bowed respectfully and exited the room.

"So, Katherine, how have you been? I can't believe your parents went on holiday with the Wellses and left you here all alone. How did you manage to talk them into allowing it?" Chloe's eyes danced.

"I'm not alone, I have Mr. Ashton to tend to me, and as you know, he has been with us for years. He wouldn't let anything happen to me." Katherine finished her tea and the maid in attendance refilled it promptly. "Thank you. So what shall we

18

do tonight? The sun will be setting soon, we could go for a swim in the pool, maybe sneak to the cellar first and grab a bottle of merlot?" The girls broke into giggles once more.

Ashton returned shortly, dressed in his formal butler's uniform as he did when the Kenningstons had an honored guest in their presence. "Your rooms are now prepared if you wish to freshen up before...swimming." He gave a vague smile indicating that he had overheard their conversation.

Teresa stood up and gave Ashton an impressive curtsy. "Thank you, Mr. Ashton. Katherine, I think that I will go up and change out of these traveling clothes if you don't mind. I will meet you and Chloe on the back patio in a few minutes." She spoke to the manservant from over her shoulder. "Mr. Ashton, if you wouldn't mind showing me to my quarters?" Ashton bowed and directed Teresa up the grand staircase that lay outside the dining room.

"Oooh, maybe they will kiss!" Chloe snickered at Rosemary.

"Do stop, you rotten thing. Mr. Ashton isn't like that, besides he doesn't like women." Katherine realized at once the tragedy in her ill-chosen statement.

Rosemary's eyes widened and she broke out in hysterical laughter. "You mean to tell me that he—"

Katherine interrupted at once, barely able to contain her own laughter. "Of course that is not what I meant! He likes women. I just meant that I have never seen him beg for the affections of one, that's all." Katherine scoffed, though she found herself somewhat interested that the thought hadn't crossed her own mind before. "Anyway, he's much too busy to care for such silly things. I'm sure that if love was of interest in him, he would have mentioned it to me at one time or another. Ashton and I have no secrets."

"At least none that you are aware of." Chloe smiled mischievously.

Katherine tossed her head back dramatically and beckoned

for her friends to follow her to the downstairs cellar to pilfer a bottle of fine wine.

The three friends reunited on the patio where Katherine poured each of them a glass of wine. Ashton arrived but didn't say anything since he knew it was all in good nature. The four girls then removed their stockings and placed their feet in the glassy black water. "Oh, Katherine, this feels absolutely wicked. Why is it that you have kept this to yourself for so long?"

Katherine smiled and turned to Ashton. She was obviously having a great time and this pleased him. She then stood and spoke frankly to Ashton. "Mr. Ashton, would you please escort me to the cellar to retrieve another bottle of merlot?"

"It would be my pleasure." Arm and arm, Ashton and Katherine walked together back to the manor, Katherine hopping along the stepping stones to not injure her delicate bare feet.

"Thank you, Ashton, this is a wonderful gift. I can't believe that you would ever imagine to be so thoughtful." She couldn't stop smiling. "Please tell me that you won't tell Mum and Father about all this; they would be dreadfully upset at me."

"Myself as well; your secret is safe with me, my dear Katherine." He opened the door to the dark cellar and lit the torch light on the wall. Katherine squinted in the dim light.

Katherine intrigued by the conversation that she had with her friends earlier, decided to nonchalantly pry for information about his past. After taking a deep breath, she inquired hesitantly about her servant's absence in love interests. "Ashton, why haven't you yet chosen a wife?" Though the previous bottle of wine had made her more bold, she found herself stunned by her own words and tried to hastily change the subject. She turned away in embarrassment. "Oh, this looks like a nice…" She reached for a large bottle on the nearby shelf.

Ashton turned to her, confused by Katherine's sudden

PRESENTLY UNTITLED

interest in his personal life. "My work is all that interests me. I made a promise to someone a long time ago that I would care for you and your parents, because of this, I don't concern myself with frivolous things such as romance." He pulled a bottle of red wine from the top shelf and handed it to her. "Does this one suit you?"

Katherine grabbed the bottle from his grasp and began to inspect it closely. "Romance, frivolous? Though I have no personal interest in falling in love, I should hardly call it frivolous. My dear Ashton, you can't possibly be serious? This is simply a job, a source of employment. You don't mean to tell me that this is your very means of interest?" Katherine dusted the bottle off with her hems, reading the label closely.

"Katherine, a gentleman such as myself who is not titled as you are, dare not to inspire to have the desire, or the time to carry on such a relation. I have come to terms with these circumstances a long time ago. Besides, my duties here satisfy me well enough."

Katherine then indicated that she had her selection of wine, feeling embarrassed by the conversation. Extinguishing the torch on the wall, Ashton led Katherine back up the darkened stairwell.

"Ashton, I hope you don't think that I was intruding. I didn't mean to be rude; curiosity sometimes gets to me as you know." Katherine found an excuse to quickly join her friends as Ashton refilled their glasses. They were soon splashing joyously at each other and before long, had to return to the house, drenched completely through.

Later that night, Katherine and her guests were drying themselves in the parlor. Ashton delivered warmed towels, and changing robes so that the girls may be comfortable. "Katherine, your servants are splendid, Mr. Ashton especially. He doesn't miss a thing!" Rosemary beamed.

"Yes, he is very special, to all of us," Katherine replied.

21

Ashton, dusting the furniture in the next room, heard this statement and smiled to himself. He knew that the Kenningstons were always very kind to him. He had no complaints about his treatment here at the manor.

They were all soon nestled in their beds sleeping comfortably in the luxury that the Kenningston manor and its staff provided. Katherine rested her head on her down pillow and found herself drifting off to sleep thinking of what a wonderful day that Ashton had made for her.

The girls awoke late that morning and enjoyed an elaborate breakfast that was served shortly before noon. As Ashton was serving, Katherine noticed a strange interaction between Ashton and Teresa. While refilling Teresa's teacup, she reached out and touched his hand gently. Ashton shockingly retracted his hand and ignored the shameless gaze that she was giving him. Katherine thought that it was strange for a grown man to ignore a woman's admirations, but figured that it had something to do with the professional code that Ashton lived by. The girls later said their goodbyes, promising to return as soon as possible and boarded the coach and went back to their respective homes.

Miss Katherine felt just as secure and content in her home as she always did in the past. Ashton served her tea at precisely the same time every day; prepared her meals at the same time every day; even fed her prized champion steed, Tom, at the very same time every day. He was unaware that she would watch him curiously from her second-story window as he tended gently to her horse after a long day's ride. He would then retire to the servant's quarters for a few hours rest, only to arise, awaiting the lady's call.

The local post boy arrived midday with word that the uprising had exceeded far beyond the limits of the city. When Miss Katherine heard word of this, she simply laughed and instructed Mr. Ashton to remove the manure from her black leather-riding boots, outwardly dismissing the importance of the message. Mr. Ashton quickly obliged, as he always did, appreciating any desire for Katherine to be ladylike. Though he knew that Katherine should know how extreme the situation was, he felt that if he gave word of what his kind were saying at the pub, it would only increase the tension at the already volatile manor. Miss Katherine didn't realize that the house servants had been aware of some type of revolt, and with the master of the house gone on holiday, it would be rather easy for the rouges to make the next head of house—Miss Kenningston, comply with their demands. Although the situation was far worse than ever, the enlightened staff felt comfortable knowing that there would be one obstacle for the lawbreakers to overcome, the honorable Mr. Ashton.

Katherine received word from the Kenningstons about mid-July. They had been having a glorious time in Cannes. Father had received word from Ashton about the revolt, though not a hint about Katherine's failed attempt at a non-permissible formal gathering. Father wrote that he had received an uncomfortable sunburn, but other than that, the voyage had been unremarkable. Mrs. Kenningston only commented on the glorious beaches and finery of the towns of France, the country that her very own parents had come from. Ashton, however, had not been his usual self these few weeks. He had been hanging about even more so than normal; in fact, he only left Miss Katherine's side when she was attending to her toiletries. Although Miss Katherine did not notice, because Mr. Ashton had always been near her side since girlhood, he had become a permanent structure in her presence. He had even taken to occasionally sleeping outside Miss Katherine's bedroom doorway to assure himself of her safety. Katherine thought little of this behavior and attributed it to nothing more than the loyalty of her long-acquainted manservant.

"Ashton, what did you do before you came to us at the manor? Your father spoke of you often, but strangely, I don't recall where he said you were." Katherine didn't turn around as she fumbled through the bookshelves looking for an appealing story she hadn't yet read.

"My apologies, milady, but I choose to keep the past just that as I had informed you before, just know that I am quite happy here tending to the manor. That is all that you need to concern yourself with." Ashton finished dusting the cherry shelves that stood before him and began polishing the brass lamps over the desk.

"I don't mean to pry, I was just curious. You know how I get. It just seems odd that I have known you for practically most of my life and yet I know nothing about you." Katherine sat sideways on the settee near the window and kicked her slippered feet comfortably onto the end table to her right.

"Uh, hum." Ashton cleared his throat in that way he always did when he wanted to correct her discreetly.

Katherine rolled her eyes and quickly sat upright imitating a more ladylike fashion. She was somewhat disturbed by the fact that Ashton didn't want to answer her question. He had never kept secrets from her before.

"There just isn't much to tell, that is all." Ashton smiled unconvincingly at Katherine.

"That's all right. I will get it out of you somehow. Annoyance is my specialty." She smiled back.

Chapter Four

IT WASN'T UNTIL THE beginning of September that
Miss Katherine noticed a change in her household. Dining had
become a less than usual event, from what was once a leg of
lamb and potatoes experience, to an elk-sausage and eggs habit.
"Why has the menu changed so?"

"It is only because of the revolt that we have experimented
with the 'local' menu, the townspeople have made it dangerous
to pass our usual route to town; therefore, we have resorted to
extraordinary means to support the manor." Sam, the stable
boy, spoke nervously.

"Whatever do you mean, the revolt hasn't transformed into
something…that serious? Why haven't I been informed?
Surely Mr. and Mrs. Kenningston explained to you that I am in
charge of the house while they are away?" The statement only
left an uneasy silence about the staff that surrounded her.
Katherine then straightened herself, and looked away, waving
her hand towards the staff members dismissively, trying

desperately to appear unattached from what was building up to be an uncomfortable situation. "Ashton, take care of this…" Head held high, she calmly headed for her sundown dip in the garden pool.

After a short but informative dialogue with the house staff, Ashton rejoined Miss Katherine at the pool with a freshly dried batch of towels and a container of perfumed powders sent from relatives in Paris. "I have spoken to the others. I will only let male service staff travel to town for supplies. It has only been ladies that have been attacked thus far; this means that you too are forbidden to go into town."

Katherine snickered at this remark. "Kind, sir, I may be but seventeen, but I assure you that I am all too aware of how these things work in this day and age, and I am certain that I, James Kenningston's daughter, am not in any danger."

Ashton shook his head, secretly having his doubts. He could not understand how harming another person could possibly appease somebody's political stance and cringed at the thought of someone harming his dearest Katherine. He was paid well to care for her and that was exactly what he intended to do, whether she liked it or not.

The next morning was the same as any at Ashton's request, kippers and eggs in the breakfast hall, then the reading by Ashton of the local newspaper in the globe room, horseback-riding by midday, and the solitary dinner and tea at sundown. Katherine was finally beginning to feel at ease with her parents away. In fact, she had begun to rather enjoy her time alone at the manor.

Nothing was changed from any other day until one of the scullery maids was seen frantically searching the manor closets. "Dear girl, whatever are you doing?" Miss Katherine stated in her usual layabout manner.

"Ann, the young servant girl, was caught in the roadway after buying cheese in town. She was beaten to nearly an inch of her life." The maid looked as though she had been crying.

Katherine could not believe that anyone would harm such a young girl. The Kenningstons had hired her, at Ashton's request, a few months past when both of her parents died unexpectedly. She would have otherwise ended up at the orphanage or possibly even at one of the town brothels. "Why on earth would she risk her life for a mere block of cheese." Katherine sneered in a manner in which imitated her parents when they were annoyed by someone's actions.

"Because, milady, you asked for it," the servant stated, matter-of-factly. Katherine looked away in embarrassment. The maid, sensing this, spoke quickly. "I am searching for towels that we may use as bandages, so if you will excuse me..." The maid hastily bowed and quickly exited the doorway.

Katherine followed to report the news to Ashton. Upon entering the room, Katherine knew that Ashton was deeply concerned.

"I must contact your father immediately," Mr. Ashton stated grimly. "He must be aware of the seriousness of our situation." He was rubbing his forehead worriedly.

"Oh, please don't. We mustn't bother them on their holiday. It will only endanger them by having them return early," Katherine retorted. She stared at him pleadingly.

"I am sorry, Miss Katherine, but I gave your father my word that I would notify him immediately if there were any issues to be dealt with at the manor while he was away. I will send post this afternoon." He walked over to the desk and began to write feverously.

Katherine was worried that her lazy summer would end prematurely, but knew that when it came to her safety, Ashton would do whatever it took to protect her. "Ashton, when will all of this end?" She could see the lines of worry all over his face. He looked as though he did not get any sleep at all that night.

Realizing her troubled look, he turned to her and spoke

softly. "Dear Katherine, your father and other local politicians have been petitioning to reduce the tax for quite some time. If only the townspeople knew that their hands were tied in this matter, the violence would stop. Until then, we must wait until the courts and Parliament make their decision." Ashton tried to conceal his concern. "You, my dear lady, mustn't worry about these things. You are safe as long as you remain in the manor. You are welcome to venture about the grounds but I must insist that you do so only if you are escorted." Katherine gave that look of disgust that she was so good at expressing, though she knew that pouting would do her no good this time. She hated to be tied down by anybody.

Though many years had passed since Katherine and Ashton had first met, Katherine remembered it as though it were yesterday. He was a tall solemn young man at the time, she remembered that he always had a forlorn look about him. She knew that he had seen hard times in his life, and figured that it must have had taken a toll on him at an early age. Jullian, the lead manservant at the time, and Ashton's father, had fallen ill with influenza and Mr. Kenningston offered the best medical services available to accommodate his longtime employee and friend's needs. Unfortunately it was to no avail and Ashton sat with his only living relative on that cold fall morning and watched him take his last breath.

Katherine remembered the day well. She had been playing in the parlor when she overheard her mother sadly tell her father that Mr. Jullian had passed. Jullian was like a member of their family, though Ashton at the time was not. Katherine had sneaked to the old man's room to take a final look at her family's lost servant, and found Ashton there at his side. Ashton was unaware of young Katherine's presence and was speaking softly to his dead father. "Don't worry about the Kenningstons, Father." His voice was shaking. "I will return this week and proudly take your place. I will send word to my headmaster immediately. I am forever indebted to them, you shall not be disappointed." Katherine, although just a child, felt nothing but sympathy and pity for the man. Though he was a large man, more so than even her father, she felt him wither at the bedside. She had only met him a few times before this, but knew that the house's elderly manservant had often spoken of him highly. He was very proud of his son and his studies at the University of London. Jullian spent his life's savings on his son's education and it was his dream for his son to become a physician.

She watched as the stoic young man grabbed his father's hand for the last time and prayed. "Dear heavenly father, please give me the strength to carry on and care for the Kenningston family and their child. Carry my father to the heavens and allow me to take his place in service to you and this household." She knew instantly that this man was just as kind and compassionate as his father was. Immediately feeling as if he could be trusted and that feeling had not left her since.

Ashton quickly adapted to the role that his father once held, and soon had the house running just as smooth as his predecessor. Mr. and Mrs. Kenningston soon grew attached to the young Ashton, almost as quick as Katherine had. It seemed that the two were inseparable from the very beginning. Ashton often seen reading to the dear child in the middle of the night, after she was awoken by her crying from one of her nightmares, or seen mending one of her dolls dresses with meticulous efficiency, teaching her how to sit at the dinner table with such etiquette that you would think she were a fine lady of the court. Mr. and Mr. Kenningston never ceased to be amazed by how Ashton had the ability to keep the young Miss Katherine in check, all the while tending to his other household duties.

Katherine spent the rest of the day reading in the globe room. She had begun to change in to her riding clothes, but was informed once again by Ashton that it was not safe to ride this late in the evening. Angrily she tossed he riding boots aside. "I will spend the rest of the evening in my quarters, if that is all right with you." She glared at him in contempt. He knew that it was hard for her to listen to him lately, since she was reaching early womanhood. She made it clear that she did not like taking orders from anyone. Ashton followed her to assist her if needed, though he did not like it when she was curt with him. He cast her one of his sideways glances and her mood soon began to soften; deep down she knew that Ashton just wanted her to be safe.

After changing into her new lace night robe that her mother had sent her from the coast, she readied herself for bed. Not knowing that she was strangely taunting the man that devoted his life to her, she twirled in front of Ashton and gave him that jokingly look that she often had. "How does it look? Mum always sends this frilly rubbish to me when she is away. I suppose it is an attempt to ready me for married life." She giggled out loud. "I don't think that I will ever be used to wearing these types of things to bed, you can see right through them…quiet drafty. Am I to be condemned for a lifetime of freezing my nip…" Ashton cleared his throat loudly once again. "…um, womanly features off?" Katherine pulled the cover over herself, oblivious to her extreme beauty. Ashton was a man, wise beyond his years, but now found it extremely hard to dismiss the grace the young woman beheld.

It just so happened that Ashton, as honorable as his attempts were, had noticed recently that Miss Katherine had blossomed into womanhood gloriously. She was no longer the girl that would attempt to climb the tallest tree in the county on a whim. Her boyish features were long gone and now only a strong willed, beautiful young woman remained. Her smoky blue eyes seemed to dance when she spoke and she was humorous by nature, which made her all the more appealing. Even in her most serious moments, she seemed to emanate happiness and jest. In his thirty-five years of life, he could not remember laying eyes on any woman quite so exquisite and was secretly ashamed that he was beginning to feel this was about someone so young. He simply pulled back the bed sheets, eyes straightforward and stated, "Will that be all for this evening, miss?"

Katherine grinned, almost knowingly aware. "Yes, Mr. Ashton, good night." She winked at him and rolled over, thinking happily of the thoughts of the day. There was a cool breeze flowing into the room that night. The fresh night air seemed to be calling to her. Crickets could again be heard in the south field chanting their song in unison.

After about an hour of struggling to fall asleep, Katherine realized that Ashton was troubled. An occasional note of music could be heard coming from the first floor below. Katherine strained, trying to hear Ashton in his quarters softly playing his piano that the Kenningstons had purchased him so many years ago. She knew that it was a kind of therapy for Ashton and he only played this passionately when he was trying to unwind, or was trying to resolve something of some importance in his own mind. Katherine listened intently to the delightful music the night air delivered to her. Smiling to herself, she could not remember when she had felt so happy and at ease, despite the latest chaos at the manor. Katherine arose to draw the curtains but stood at the window, gazing at the night sky. She hummed softly to the glorious sounds that were lifted to her ears. She eventually focused her attentions to the night sky that was lit with hundreds of twinkling stars. It would be the last full moon of the summer, the last time that she would be so fully illuminated by this mysterious and distant planet. She soon found herself saddened at the thought of leaving the manor. The days of moonlight swims, and running barefoot through the manor gardens would soon be over. And strangely worst of all, the days of running about with Ashton watching over her every move, would be soon ending.

Continuing her dreamlike state, she stared at the slow

rolling fields that lay before her. After a few moments of basking in this scenery, her eyes shifted lazily to the white wooden stables; tonight would indeed be a glorious night for a ride. Ashton was distracted at the moment and she would surely not be in danger on a night as perfect as this. Quickly, before she had a chance to change her mind, she pulled on her robes, and traveled to the main floor by means of the formal stairway. Picking up the hems of her nightgown, she took flight down the slate-grey marble stairs, praying that she would not be discovered. Knowing that if she used the servant's stairwell, which was the quickest route to the stables, Ashton or the other house staff would surely notice her. She definitely did not want to be lectured again this evening.

Katherine stepped out onto the stone patio, which directly led to the stables, basking in the exuberant nightfall. She had to relentlessly concentrate on retaining her sudden explosion of giggles. She stopped momentarily, breathlessly listening to the sound of the piano that could still be heard through Ashton's open window, assuring her that she had escaped unnoticed. After saddling her horse, she found herself trotting at top speed through the west pasture. The soft feeling of the field below her seemed to be even more of a reason to ride onward. Though the night was slightly chilly, she hadn't a care in the world and even her horse seemed to feel it. She rode freely with her long hair flowing carelessly behind her, forgetting about what would happen if anyone from the house caught her. Freedom. That is all that she is thinking about tonight. The moon cast glorious shadows on the fresh grass beneath her and she could smell the heavenly sweet scent of wheat grass and wildflowers from the distant meadow.

After many minutes of riding, Katherine stopped by the slow running stream that divided the pastures from the forest, placing her bare feet in the crisp water. She smiled to herself as she remembered that Ashton had once taught her to fish in this very stream as a child. Her horse drank thirstily while she sat at the water's edge throwing stones, taking in the fresh night air. She heard dogs barking at the neighboring estate, but did not bother with it as she oftentimes heard them from the house.

As she arose to return to her steed, she heard a faint inaudible whisper from behind the large oak bordering the forest. "Who's there?"

Katherine, assuming that her ears were playing tricks on her, was suddenly very aware that she was parading around in the night air with nothing on but her nightclothes and robe. If word got back to her parents, or worse, Ashton, she would surely be confined to the house for the rest of the summer. She giggled at the prospect of being the center of the local rumor... 'Miss Katherine, a woman the utmost wealth and class...spotted riding bareback in nothing but her underclothes...she surely has gone mad!' She could imagine the sharp remarks that Mrs. Wells and the other parish members would have to say about that.

Katherine was suddenly overcome with the dark feeling that someone was watching her. "Who's there?" She once again heard the whispers from within the forest though she could not see anyone. Her heart felt as if it were beating in her throat and she suddenly had a heavy feeling in the pit of her stomach. She quickly returned to her horse casting an occasional furtive glance over her shoulder as she walked. From behind the tree line she saw a dark shadow approaching quickly. She felt her feet take flight as she reached for her saddle strap. Just as she began to mount her horse, she was grabbed from behind and pulled to the ground, her face sharply hitting the stones below. She screamed in terror as she felt herself being dragged further into the darkened tree line.

Realizing that she was now surrounded be three fully-grown men in dirty farm clothes, she began kicking and screaming with all of her strength. The darkness of the forest made it nearly impossible for her to identify her captors. "Help me! Oh dear God! Somebody!" Her voice was hoarsened from the intensity of her screams. She heard the men coldly laugh at her pleas. They knew that they were much too far from the house for anyone to hear and their grip tightened painfully. "What do you want from me!" she cried as they dragged her by her wrists along the forest floor. She felt twigs break beneath her and tear at her skin, the sting of her abrasions keeping her from fainting with fright.

Though she could not see his face clearly, she heard one of the indistinguishable men state gruffly, "We are going to get a little tax of our own." The other two men smiled, baring their broken and yellowed teeth.

She knew at once that the tallest of the three men was Timothy Barnes, a boy whose father had once been a coachman of the family. He was fired after he was caught stealing from the cold storehouse. "Timothy, please, it is I, Katherine, surely you remember me? How could you do this?" He only glared at her. Suddenly, she felt a searing pain at the back of her head, then a warm trickle of blood down her shoulder soaking the remains of her nightgown. The voices seemed to be distant now, and her vision began to blur, only the steady throb of her heart pounding in her ears assured her that she was still, for the moment, alive. She felt herself being thrown face first over a large fallen tree; the rough, dry bark embedding itself into her fragile skin. She was attempting to fight the men off, but was drifting in and out of consciousness. Suddenly the third man approached her from behind; she knew at that point that her girlhood was gone forever. As each man took his turn she prayed for death.

As her vision once again began to fade, there were the familiar sounds of hooves nearby. Shortly thereafter a muzzle blast was heard in the distant recesses of her mind. She once again drifted into the blissful darkness that was protecting her, this time not waking up so quickly.

When Ashton had done his nightly rounds of the house that evening, he found Miss Katherine's bed empty. Glimpsing the cool moonlight flooding beaming from the large windows, he knew at once that she had gone riding—unescorted. His heart filled with alarm. As he searched the stables realizing her horse was absent, he heard Katherine's frantic screams from somewhere in the distance.

Preparing his muzzleloader en route, he was ready for nearly anything except for what he was about to see. He arrived as the last man was brutally finishing with her. His anger flared at the abuse that his dear Katherine had just experienced. He thought she was dead when he saw her blood-soaked hair covering her face. Quickly, he fired with amazing accuracy at the man nearest to her and he fell to the ground, dead. The other two men wrestled Ashton from his stallion. In a flurry of blood and fists, the two remaining men were overcome by Ashton's strength and fled into the night.

Katherine tried to stand, drunkenly searching for any shred of dignity, covering her nearly bare body with the bits of cloth that remained of her nightclothes. She was mumbling incoherently and had a lost look about her. Horrified by the sight of her own blood, she looked toward Ashton and began screaming. She held her bloodied hands out before her and just stared at them, screaming. Her attentions soon turned to the dead man that lay at Ashton's feet. It was as if suddenly she could not find her own voice. She just stared with her mouth wide, opening and closing as if she were gasping for air. In this moment of silence, she dropped to her knees and sighed in her own grief. She then looked at her rescuer and whispered in a childlike voice. "Ashton, my dearest friend, they've killed me." She then fell limply to the ground, unconscious.

Ashton removed his overcoat and placed it on her as he lifted her bruised body to his horse, blood soaking his white cotton butler's shirt. With nothing but the moon to guide the way, he returned to the manor quickly and quietly. "You can breathe easy now, dear Katie, we'll be home soon. Just stay with me." He whispered to her any words of encouragement that he could think of, not knowing if she was even alive to hear them. Though he rode frantically, he could occasionally see her beautiful face beneath the heavy overcoat. Despite the blood drying on her cheek, it appeared as if she were sleeping in the moonlight that illuminated her. He rode at top speed to the manor, fearing the worst, that Katherine may be mortally wounded. He cursed to himself for allowing such a thing to happen to the girl that he devoted his life to protect and care for.

After a few short moments, Ashton was safely within the gray walls of the manor. Carrying her to her quarters, he placed Katherine in her bed and carefully inspected her limp body for any critical wounds. It was then that he reported the attack to the house staff, instructing them not to enter the room, for any reason, until the lady of the house was comfortable. He carried a basin of warm water and clean towels to her bedside, where he replaced her ruined nightgown and washed all signs of the evening's tragic events from her body. Katherine slept soundly while Ashton tended to her, applying ointment to her lacerations, and placing cool compresses on the large lump at the back of her head. It was then, weakened by his own wounds, that he collapsed to the floor in a pool of blood.

Chapter Five

SUNRISE FLOODED THE ROOM with glorious pink light and awoke Katherine with a start. Although her memory was somewhat foggy, she knew at once by the sharp pains between her legs what had undoubtedly happened. "Ashton?" Her voice was raspy and coarse. Her eyes had trouble focusing and there was a deafening throb at the back of her head. "Ashton, where are you?"

Liz, the lead maid, entered the room and curtseyed. "Can I help you, miss?" Katherine stared at the starchy dressed maid, bewildered.

"Where is Mr. Ashton? I must speak with him right away." Katherine could feel the large lump throbbing at the back of her head.

Liz's pudgy pink face became grim. She gave Katherine a deeply accusing look that confused Katherine. She squinted at the bright sunlight that was blinding her trying to shield the light with her hand.

SARA DE ARMON

"He was badly injured in the attack last night. I've already sent for a doctor, but it may have been of no use since the roads are still blocked." Before the maid had even finished her sentence, Katherine had weakly pulled on her robe and began the descent down the servant's stairwell. She grasped the polished oak rail firmly to steady herself as she approached the main floor. Once again, she felt faint but continued towards her wounded attendee's room. Katherine knew that Ashton's quarters were directly behind the kitchens and storage area because she had once been caught indulging herself in the cream pies as a young girl. Ashton, rather than worry the master of the house, invited the child into his quarters where he gave a lengthy lecture on honesty and stealing. Katherine had not been to this part of the manor since.

As she walked into the dimly lit room, she immediately gasped at the sight of Ashton in his bed. The man, whom she had always regarded to be a very strong man, looked weak and helpless beneath the coarse cotton sheets. His face was deadly pale, and his lips had taken on a bluish tinge.

She grasped his cold hand and desperately cried, "Ashton, what have they done to you!" Tears were streaming down her face. She kissed his cold hand, desperate for any movement or signs of life from her dear servant. Sensing Liz behind her, she turned and spoke rapidly. "I don't understand, what has happened to him? He saved me, how did he get these injuries?"

"He has taken a dreadful stab to his kidney, miss. We can only hope that he will make it to see nightfall." Liz glared at Katherine.

"I don't understand, what is going on?" Katherine could sense the anger from the maid.

Liz pointed an accusing finger at the young Katherine and spoke curtly. "The next time some rogues try to lift your coin purse, you had very well give it up obligingly!" The servant was trembling with despise.

Katherine, still dazed from her head injury, stared at the

maid confused. "My coin purse?" Katherine replied, bewildered by the maid's odd statements.

"Yes, your coin purse, you are far beyond lucky that those men didn't have their way with you. Ashton told us before he collapsed just how grave things were. If it weren't for Mr. Ashton risking his dear life to save your skin, they very well may have had their run about you." Liz trotted out of the room, clearly brimming with fury.

Katherine called for the menservants of the house and instructed them to move Mr. Ashton to her quarters on the second floor. The large bed was far more comfortable and therefore befitting of a man with his extent in injuries. The house was quiet with the sorrow that they shared for their dear fallen Ashton. Only the occasional servant would be seen entering the room to care for Ashton, trying carefully to awaken him, to show any signs of improvement in his health. It was there that Katherine sat beside him in her cushioned armchair, softly reading from her latest mail-order novels. Katherine only left the room when the housemaids tended to his wounds. When the maids and attendees would leave, she would return to his side and begin to read, all the while thinking of the happy days, weeks, and years that she had spent with her dear Ashton.

The days wore on and still Katherine remained by his side. The immense guilt and responsibility of his injuries began to take its toll on her. She vowed that she would not leave his side until he was nearly recovered. That day came none too soon.

After taking a moment to rest her weary eyes, Katherine could not help but to notice Ashton's large muscular build. She simply had not noticed his striking handsomeness before since she had never seen him out of his formal butler's garments. In fact, she hadn't even seen him with so much as his shirtsleeves rolled up. His usually tidy hair was now moist with perspiration and clung to his face in dark wavy locks.

Ashton was having a fitful sleep, more than once startling Katherine by screaming out "Katie! They've got my Katie!" He would then shut his dark brown eyes and return to his restless state. Katherine knew that 'Katie' was a name that he called her as a child and didn't quite understand why he was calling out for her by this name. It wasn't until she had began to bloom and parade around at parties, at her parents' request, in all her finery that Mrs. Kenningston insisted she bear her given name. Mrs. Kenningston knew that, though as modern as she was, Katherine would never fetch a decent suitor with a name like 'Katie.'

The following night droned on, much like the last. Katherine continued pressing cool cloths to Ashton's forehead in effort to fight off the fever and arranging the pillows beneath him to make him more comfortable. He had acquired an infection in his wound, which had added to his already compromised condition.

Morning abruptly came and still no word from the town physician. Katherine was beginning to fear the worst for her dear companion. Delirious with lack of sleep, she bent closely to his ear and spoke softly to him, pleading. "Ashton, please wake up. You have been my closest friend for years. You know my deepest secrets; I can't imagine what I will do without you by my side. Please come back." She brushed his dark hair from his fevered forehead. A feeling of sadness that she hadn't experienced before crept over her. She hadn't realized how much Ashton had meant to her until now. Ashton's role in her life was far more important to her than she had ever thought.

As Katherine tried to wet her servant's parched lips with water in a spoon, Ashton slowly opened his eyes and tried to speak but his voice failed him. "Shh, don't speak, you must save your energy, dear man." Katherine soothed him with more water and frantically called for Liz to inform her of his awakening.

"Liz! He's awakened! Ashton has awakened!" Liz was soon

at his bedside checking him over, testing the strength of his pulse and temperature of his forehead.

"I think that the worst is over. I'll fetch him some broth. He will need nourishment to strengthen him." The maid was gone in a flash and Katherine buried her face in her hands and cried. She had never been so thankful in her life.

When Liz left the room, Katherine kissed Ashton tenderly on the forehead. She wanted to hold him and soothe him. Nothing else but him mattered to her in the world.

Chapter Six

THREE DAYS LATER, ASHTON was permitted to leave the comforts of Katherine's room, but at Katherine's strict request was only allowed to walk with assistance nearby. The fever had weakened him greatly and slowed his recovery, though he strived not to show it. Katherine had taken the role that Ashton once played serving and caring for him with the utmost of concern, rarely leaving his side. He often pleaded for her to leave him but Katherine simply gave him that stern look she always gave when she was not going to back down. It was while having tea in the garden that Ashton and Katherine received word that the lady and lord of the house would be returning in two days, bringing a physician. "Isn't this wonderful! Maybe the doctor will have something that will help heal your wound."

Ashton did not appear particularly overjoyed at the idea. "I assure you that I am healing more than adequately, miss. I don't think that you should fret so much about me."

Though Ashton was nearly recovered, Katherine persuaded him to at least have the good doctor take a look at his wounds. Katherine had recovered fully without so much as a scar to remind her of her tragic night, though emotionally, she would never be the same. The local authorities had no leads to who perpetrated the attack.

It was during dinner that night that Katherine sent for Ashton to join her. She had decided that since he was looking healthier, and her parents were due to return soon, it was time to speak of the horrific event that she had endured. Ashton usually stood just inside the lavish dining room entrance, awaiting any task that his employers endeavored him, but his current state only allowed him to sit at a nearby bench because he had not fully regained his strength. Bewildered, and openly uncomfortable with Katherine's request, Ashton joined her at the grand oak table. He straightened his jacket, smoothed his hair, and sat directly across from the fair lady Katherine, all the while finding it difficult to look her in the eyes.

Katherine's voice trembled and her eyes reddened with the tears she tried to hold back as she addressed him formally. "Mr. Ashton, there are a few things yet that puzzle me regarding the dealings of the past few weeks. I guess that I should just get right to the point. The night of the…attack, why did you tell the house staff that the quarrel was over my coin purse? Surely you noticed that I was in my nightclothes and my coin purse wasn't anywhere in my possession?" Her large eyes filled with tears that she wiped with her napkin. She had attempted to speak with Ashton in a calm, up-front tone but her fierce emotions got the better of her.

"Yes, milady." A long silence followed as he arose slowly from his high-backed dining chair and closed the dining room doors to dissuade any eavesdroppers. He returned and seated himself, once again smoothing his black servant's jacket, something that he did when he was nervous. He breathed deeply before he replied. "It was the only thing that I could think of in my haste that would explain the situation while keeping your virtue…intact." His eyes soon drifted to the floor in embarrassment for his actions and for what had happened to her. "Your coming-out ball is a mere four weeks away and an event such as this one, happening to a lady of your status and honor, well I imagine would be…devastating."

Her temper flared immediately. "You hardly think that I am going to pursue any suitors now that I've been spoiled!" The tears were flowing freely down her face at this point. Her teenage emotions were often out of her control, but it seemed that they were increasing more as of late. "I shall never find a proper husband because of my thoughtlessness! Did you really believe that my future husband would not know that I have been ruined long before my wedding night!" She could barely speak the words between sobs.

Ashton spoke gently to the saddened Katherine. "Miss Katherine, I am a man who has seen and experienced many things. I can only hope that you will understand what I am about to explain to you." He continued speaking softly to Katherine, hoping to somehow find a way to ease her young, weary heart. "For thousands of years mankind has been befuddled with the workings of a woman's body. It is highly unlikely that a newly wed groom would notice such a detail, or even give it a second thought, if given a proper explanation. The extent of knowledge these boys have of women and their workings is owed almost entirely to the town whores and that is hardly a significant or reputable source of information. I was merely trying to make things easier in your own mind by lying. It is not my place to speak of such things without your consent. And quite frankly, I felt that an ordeal such as that one would be just too painful for a woman of your tender age to relive in words. I must admit that I am a tad overprotective of you at times, I suppose that I was hoping that we could get you through this thing without any embarrassment for you." He was seriously doubting his actions were correct at this point. "I was also trying to save your family from any undue and unjust snickerings from the town's socialites. If you wish to tell of what has happened to you, so be it. I was only trying to ensure that the words came from your mouth and not the town gossip. Now, if you will excuse me, miss."

He bowed and painfully grimacing as he returned to his post at the doorway. He knew that Katherine was much too young to realize that this would, as with all difficult things, be someday be in the past. Though he could only imagine how terrible it must be for someone of such a tender age to endure, he was also hurt that she was acting so coldly towards him. Katherine quietly finished her meal and then announced to Ashton that she was ready to retire for the evening. He escorted her to her room where he prepared her for bed, all the while trying not to appear bothered by her criticisms from earlier.

Mr. and Mrs. Kenningston arrived early on Sunday in a flurry of baggage and gifts for the staff. They arrived with the county's best physician, but Ashton changed his mind and insisted that he leave at once, insuring the Kenningstons that he was in optimal health. Mrs. Kenningston was relieved to see that Katherine had nearly recovered from the barbaric attack. She would have many stories to tell at her next country club event. Katherine decided that it was best for now not to include the dark details of what really happened, for fear of worrying her mother into a panic. One man was already dead from the incident, two at large. She knew that her father would spend every last hour of his life searching for the men who wronged her and she now desperately needed her parents' undivided attention. The autumn ball was almost upon them.

It was later that day after the Kenningstons had unpacked that they began to question their daughter's caretaker. "Ashton, my dear man. How ever did you manage to rescue my dear Katie from those rogues?" Mr. Kenningston inquired while

Ashton served him his morning tea.

Ashton felt somewhat apprehensive speaking about the subject, and tried to keep the matter short. "It was a stroke of luck that I managed to take the first man down with one shot. They were all taken by surprise. The town authorities have yet to determine who the dead man was. Strangely, there hasn't even been any family in to identify him."

Ashton's memory of that night pained him to think about though he strained to appear indifferent. He continued to have flashbacks of the beautiful Katherine splayed naked over a tree, begging for mercy.

"Well, I guess I don't need to explain how much I thank you for saving my little miss." Mr. Kenningston slapped Ashton hard on the shoulder and he nearly collapsed with the pain in his back. Though he wanted everyone to believe that he had healed completely, he was having a difficult time with recovering not only from his wound, but the painful memories of what he had seen that night.

"Thank you. I just didn't want anything to happen to our dear Katherine. She is such a free spirit at times!" Ashton tried to jokingly dismiss the whole thing. Mr. Kenningston laughed and Ashton was far too familiar with what Mr. Kenningston had meant. Her determination to have free will had ultimately cost her dearly.

Ashton readied the coach and escorted Miss Katherine to town. There wasn't much time for preparation for the ball since her parents' arrival, and there were gowns to fit, perfumes to sample, flowers to choose to her liking. The country club hall was chosen for the gala; this was the place that almost all of the town's most important festivities were and only those arraigned in the highest regard of the socialites and their escorts were able to attend for most of these occasions. There were five girls who would be on display, announcing their coming of age and all hoped to find someone to marry that evening as some of their mothers, aunts, sisters had before them. This was a tradition that had been carried on for many generations and it was always an event surrounded by fanciful things and splendor. It was considered one of the most important events in a young girl's life.

Katherine soon began to feel like the young woman she should be, putting the adult scenes that she had terribly endured in her past. She had simply pretended that the whole thing had never happened. Ashton was no longer limping about the house, and had appeared to regain his usual masculine, yet often quiet, composure. It was he, who, in fact, helped make the final decision on the dress that she was to wear. Katherine was desperate to have a man's opinion, and Ashton had always had a fashionable sense when it came to choosing clothing for Katherine's events.

The day was a breath of fresh air to Katherine and her servant and they were both enjoying their day away from the routines of the manor. Both were seen laughing ceaselessly at the flower shop, choosing fresh blooms to her liking, though some were obviously chosen simply to see which could make the other laugh the hardest. Their joking manner had the shop owners and attendants smiling at the sight of the two. It was as if the two had been best friends all of their lives.

Katherine had a way of making Ashton feel years younger than he was. He had missed out on many of the jovial years of his youth due to the unexpected death of his mother and then soon later, his father. He had to grow up long before he could enjoy any of the exciting events that the other young gentlemen attended.

While in the many fine garment shops, Katherine would politely not allow any of the lady shopkeepers assist her in trying their wares. She had grown to distrust anybody but Ashton and her parents, though no one but Ashton knew why. Mrs. Kenningston guessed that it was a normal phase that a girl of her age was going to go through and thought no more of the matter. The shop attendants were quite aware of Ashton's loyalty to the Kenningston family and therefore didn't mind letting him handle the lady's needs.

They finally decided upon a blushing pale pink dress with sweeping neckline and tight bodice. Though the dress had an air of innocence about it, somehow, in the way that it conformed to her body, it made even the shopkeeper blush. It was not improper in any way but just had a feeling of sheer sexuality bursting from it that made everyone turn and admire the way it fit her. The undergarments were made of the sheerest silk woven in India and gently plumed her hems out so that she appeared to be walking on air. Katherine, though not always concerned with the luxuries of pretty items, seemed to be fascinated with the unique style of this particular garment. Ashton couldn't help but to be taken aback when he assisted her into these luxurious clothes because she was positively stunning. His heart sank when she began fretting about which boy she shall dance with first, which to invite for tea. He would never admit this to himself, but he secretly wished she were talking about him.

He soon felt confused with how he felt about the girl that he was paid to tend and care for. Ashton, whom had devoted his life to his work, and had never known true love for a woman, but something, had begun to change within him. There was an unknown feeling deep within Ashton at that moment, a feeling that resembled jealousy. Though he knew that one day Katherine would be leaving, he didn't realize until now that the time was now almost upon them.

Ashton found himself wanting Katherine, in a way unbecoming of a man—and especially, a servant. Though he had cared for her since girlhood, he could not help but to feel fury in his heart when he thought about any man touching her. He still found himself awakening during the night, in a cold sweat, screaming her name. He tried to dismiss these sensations of trauma due to seeing her attackers ravaging her body before his very eyes. But there was still something else, something that a man feels for a woman, despite their age and social differences. She had changed before his very eyes. There was suddenly a difference in the way she walked, a gracefulness in her movements and the things that she said, that he had not noticed before. There was also something in her eyes that made him forget, though just for a moment, who and what he was.

"Ashton, have you not heard a word I have said?" Katherine was waving her hand before his eyes as if to awaken him from a trance.

Ashton realized that he was indeed someplace else and apologized. "Terribly sorry, Miss Katherine. I guess I was just lost in thought." He found himself embarrassed that she had discovered he was daydreaming and searched for something to draw the attention away from himself. "Let's have the shop assistant box up these items immediately and head for the manor, shall we? It will be getting dark soon." Ashton excused himself and began shouting commands at the shop owner on how to package the items in a way so that they do not wrinkle as much.

The next week seemed like an eternity. With the many preparations for the ball, Katherine found herself exhausted, strangely more so than usual. She remained in her bed for most of almost every morning, only rising when Ashton would call for her. One morning she had even requested that Ashton only bring her some toast and tea for breakfast in her room. Mrs. Kenningston rambled about the house in hysterics, prepping the coachmen on what to wear, brushing up on some of proper ways to escort a lady to a ball such as this.

"Ashton, whatever is the matter with Katherine? She has been in her room sleeping for most of the day and when I went up to tell her that her flowers had arrived, she looked positively pale!" Ashton also had concerns with Katherine's health, noticing that she seemed somehow different. She was moody and lethargic for most of this week and could laugh hysterically and then cry in just a matter of minutes. Mrs. Kenningston, though a loving and caring mother, had usually bestowed much of the parenting and care taking of her only child to Ashton. She was very busy with her social duties in her church, women's club, and being a member of the town's elite class required her to often travel with Mr. Kenningston on some wealthy business trip or another.

"Yes, she hasn't been herself lately. I have been concerned also." His face was grim.

"Do you think that maybe she is still suffering from the shock of her attack this summer?" For just a moment, Ashton contemplated on whether or not to tell Mrs. Kenningston everything. He decided once again, that it should be Katherine's decision to tell her parents about the dreadful occurrence she narrowly survived. "It is most likely just the excitement of the ball. I will speak to her immediately." Ashton excused himself and quickly went upstairs.

Ashton knocked lightly and entered the room. The soft scent of fresh cut roses filled the air. The sunshine poured in through the lace curtains and warmed her still body. Ashton cleared his throat loudly, hoping that she would awaken on her own. Katherine stirred slightly and promptly fell back to sleep. "Miss Katherine?" He spoke softly. "I am sorry to awaken you, but your mother was inquiring about your behavior as of late, and I thought that I might have a word with you...to see how you are doing." He took a step closer to her large canopied bed. Nearly completely naked, she looked like an angel beneath the cream-colored imported sheets with the glow of the light around her. His heart and mind once again found themselves lost in some distant daydream.

Katherine peered at him through sleepy eyes. "Oh, Ashton, why do you always fret so?" As she rolled over he could make out the silhouette of her body beneath the sheets. She noticed his glance and gave him a quizzical look. "Really, Mr. Ashton, what has gotten into you? You've been sulking around the manor like you've lost your best friend... Oh, that's it, isn't it?" She smiled lazily at the hulky servant. "Don't worry, dear, you will be more than welcome to come into my employment when I have become the future Mrs. Whoever." Katherine sighed loudly then turned over and continued her nap. The words burned like fire in Ashton's heart. Katherine had become quite accustomed to having whatever she wanted and didn't always put other people's feelings on her priority list.

With no explanation to the way he felt, Ashton simply replied, "Thank you for this consideration, miss," and left the room solemnly.

Chapter Seven

THE NIGHT OF THE ball finally came. Ashton spent most of the afternoon removing and replacing the curling rolls to Miss Katherine's auburn hair. Katherine speaking so excitedly that Ashton, chuckling to himself, had trouble understanding. Her youthful conversation was always a pleasing to him. He was always so involved with his work that, other than an occasional visit to the pub, he took little time out for himself to socialize. It was his devotion to his work that ultimately stood in the way of him choosing a wife.

As Katherine stood before him, in her naked essence preparing to be placed in her undergarments, Ashton felt, for the first time in his life, a real desire and longing for a woman. Though he had known Katherine since she was a girl collecting frogs from the cow pond, it now took all of his strength not to reach out and touch her, to caress her every curve. He refrained from looking directly at her in an effort to make things easier on himself, but inadvertently brushed against her bosom as he was tightening her petticoats. He had to instantly turn his attentions downward and intently focus on arranging her laces in efforts to not make his thoughts obvious. She was stunning, absolutely breathtaking. All the while she was chatting ceaselessly about the latest bachelor boys, or what they will have at the buffet, he was suffocating with her beauty right before her, and she didn't even know it. Every word, every whisper was like someone was grasping his heart and lungs, forbidding him to breathe. Just the way that she gave that sideways smile to him when she was speaking of something out of taste, made him wish that life were somehow different. Made him wish that he himself were different. If only entitlement was not a requirement in relationships of this regard, things would be different. He would tell her how he felt and not be ashamed of who he was.

She paused, noticing the distant forlorn look on Ashton's face and then spoke to him carefully. "Ashton, I do want to apologize about what I said the other day. That nonsense about being in my employ… I know I don't often tell you these kinds of things, but you are truly my best friend. You have stood by me in my darkest times…and now you stand before me in my very best. I want you to know that which ever choice I make in these next few weeks, you are welcome in my household…as a friend."

Ashton tilted his chin upward, an effort to appear distanced and replied, "That is very kind of you, miss. I would be divinely honored," he lied. Ashton knew that if he so much as stepped foot into a place where his dear Katherine and her future spouse slept, he would surely die of a broken heart.

He turned to Miss Katherine's vanity table and grabbed the specialty perfume; the perfume that she wanted him to pick out. He, though Katherine was unaware, chose the scent because it reminded him of the long summer days that they would spend in the meadows catching butterflies, grasshoppers, in the days when things were still…simple. He did not like preparing this perfect woman before him, for someone else. He turned to her and applied the smallest amount of fragrance to her earlobes, noticing the softness of her neck and shoulders. He suddenly thought of the many memories that were soon to be forgotten, brushed aside as if they hadn't even existed. Trying to desperately remove these thoughts from his mind, he focused on the gently curve of her cheek. As he was doing so, Katherine's eyes met his. There was a strange stillness in the air around the room. Though neither of them knew what the other was thinking, both felt as if time stood still, just for a moment. He could gaze into her blue-gray eyes forever just as she could stare into his in return.

"Hurry up, you two! The coachmen are ready!" It was as though the two of them had just been awoken from a trance, lost in some faraway place.

Ashton once again turned away, hoping to hide his shame for the way he felt. An entrusted manservant having thoughts and feelings for his master's daughter, it was unspeakable. "Here are your gloves, Miss Katherine, try not to spill anything on them. And do not, for any reason, remove them, it is considered impolite. I don't care how uncomfortable they are." Katherine swatted him jokingly on the shoulder. He quickly assisted Miss Katherine into her gloves, gave her a few last minute tips, and then hurried her out of the room feeling as if he was giving away his life's treasure. When Katherine reached the top of the staircase, she glanced over her shoulder to Ashton, and once again found herself deeply staring at him, dismissing the look that he had given her earlier as just a friendly gesture.

Katherine felt as if she were a bride already, on display for all to see. The dress that Ashton had chosen was as though it were designed especially for her. It accented every curve and every movement that she made seemed effortless. As she descended the main stairs, the house staff gathered to see her in all of her splendor. Ashton walked beside her gently guiding her by her arm while she held up her hems with her high-gloved hand. Nothing could be heard at that moment but the delicate rustle of her dress as she approached the main floor. Katherine felt nervous and gazed around, confused as to why everyone was staring at her so. The imported fragrance of her perfume softened the air so perfectly around them that even the coachmen were bedazzled.

"My dear daughter, just look at you! You look like a little princess. Do try to have fun tonight and remember, no dabbling in the rum!" Mr. Kenningston beamed.

Mrs. Kenningston, standing at his side, was wiping her eyes discreetly with her handkerchief. She sniffled once and hugged her daughter. "You just look so grown up. I'm certain that you will be the prettiest girl there. Enjoy yourself." She turned to Ashton and smiled. "Take care of my little miss. See that those boys don't try to be anything but gentlemen in my daughter's presence." She then hugged Ashton and wished him luck also. "You had better stop smiling so handsomely or you just might return home married yourself!" Everyone except for Ashton laughed.

They traveled the long trip into town to the country club with barely a word to be spoken. Katherine stared out the window nearly the entire trip, clearly lost in her thoughts. They were both unknowingly engrossed in their thoughts about the feelings that they were having for each other, though neither one was going to admit it. While Katherine could once tell anything to her dear Ashton, she found it difficult to speak to him about anything lately because of the strange feeling that overcame her when she spoke to him. Unknowingly, this was going to be a difficult night for both of them. Katherine's thoughts drifted to how dangerous it was to travel this late at night; the men that attacked her were unfound and the village farming community were still revolting against the new tax.

Nevertheless, she felt like a queen and her court. With the four coachmen and Ashton to escort her, she knew that nothing could dampen her evening.

Katherine noticed early in the evening how Ashton was stunning in his three-piece tailored suit and silken hair smoothed back with a fragrant pomade. Katherine loved to see Ashton out of his familiar butler's garb, though it was rare. He could easily pass as one to the township's elite in his fancy attire and handsome face. As they rode in silence, she reached out and held her beloved Ashton's hand, seeking comfort and confidence. She needed, this night more that ever, Ashton's reassurance and encouragement. Though he did not like the idea of someone else admiring his dear Katherine, he knew that it was to be her destiny to marry a gentleman that could properly care for her. This gentleman was not to be him.

They arrived at the country club in record time. Ashton gave Katherine's silky hair a quick toss, and then helped her out of the coach.

"It's beautiful," Katherine gasped as she stared at the country club.

"I will agree with you there, my dear." Ashton never appeared to be uncomfortable at these types of events though she secretly knew that he was. He always had that calm air about him in any situation that amazed Katherine.

The country club was lit up like New Year's Eve. There were lanterns glowing in every corner and along the cobblestone walkway. Large pink and white ribbons were tied around each of the grand oaks that marked the entrance of the elite hall and bouquets representing each girl were displayed at the entrance. An orchestra could be heard playing gaily inside, beckoning them indoors. The partygoers' voices within were happy and excited.

As Ashton walked Katherine formally down the pathway to the entrance, he noticed an unusual change in her walk.

Unexpectedly, he felt Katherine gently begin to sway. Quickly grasping her arm, he tried to steady her, thinking she had simply tripped over a stone. He then realized that she had a dazed look in her eyes and caught her around the waist just as she began her quick descent to the hard stone path.

"Katherine? Miss Katherine, please wake up," he whispered loudly to her, trying to not attract any attention to the two of them. Her heavy lidded eyes began to open as he held her ever close to his body. He was suddenly aware of how perfect she felt in his arms, despite the unusual circumstances, as she seemed to melt within his very grasp.

"Katherine, milady, are you all right?" Her eyes then opened completely, slowly finding his. Once again, he found her awakening as if in a dream state. His heart begging to prolong this moment of closeness that they shared for just a second longer, before he had to place her on that altar to be given to the highest bidder.

Her confusion soon faded as she looked up at him confusedly and stated, "Yes, of course. What happened?" Still holding her, he could see the sleepy look in her eyes.

"I'm afraid you've fainted." He continued to hold her warm body against his. He could sense that she was regaining the strength in her knees.

"Fainted?" she replied, fighting to stand upright. "What on earth for?" The color began to return to her cheeks as she began angrily brushing off her hem and petticoats.

Ashton looked at her gravely. "We have probably just bound your dress up too tight and with all of this excitement it was more than you could handle." Forcing a smile, he had fears and doubts of his own, but convinced himself that what he stated was true.

"Oh, I see. Well, let's get on, shall we?" She continued, though flushed, as if nothing had happened. Ashton tightened his grip on her arm, feeling just as nervous inside as Katherine appeared on the outside.

As they entered the main hall arm in arm, they stopped ceremoniously and awaited their announcement. Ashton straightened himself into a formal stance, grasping her arm distantly in the formal way that the servants were taught. He could sense Katherine was holding her breath, apparently both aware this was the moment they had been preparing for. At last they heard, "Announcing...Miss Katherine Kenningston, escorted by Mr. Ashton Williams!" Everyone clapped and the music resumed. Ashton seated Katherine at the table with the other four ladies who would be announced tonight, all dressed in dazzling proper gowns. His large hand discreetly patted Katherine's shoulder, comforting her. He then took his place behind her chair, eyes straight forward, hands folded behind his back as he and the other servants were instructed. The waiters then brought out the dining carts and began serving the attendees superb feast.

During the meal, Katherine cheerfully discussed the latest topics with the other young ladies. Unfortunate for Katherine, politics were at the top of the topic list of everyone that evening. She knew that her father's political stance was in accord with the other girls' fathers and feared that it would be the highlighted topic in which she found ultimately, given her circumstances, disturbing. She soon confirmed her fears when Teresa began the conversation. "I just don't know what the poor want us to do about the latest tax increase. It's not like we, ourselves, asked for it. I say that if they want to continue to use our land, they had better just deal with it and pay up."

"I agree, it isn't our fault that we were born entitled. You would think it was a sin, by the way they are behaving. It's atrocious!" Rosemary sighed out loud.

Katherine spoke up at once, praying that she could rapidly change the subject. "Can we talk about something else? I would much rather talk about Sir Lawrence's perfectly fitting jacket and trousers, if you know what I mean?" The girls giggled out loud, while staring across the room at the crowd of young men at the bar. They were soon served seafood cocktail and the club's finest wines.

One of Katherine's close friends, Teresa, was also being presented this night. She was a tall slender girl, regarded as very pretty. She would have no difficulties finding a suitor this evening. They laughed as they shared memories of the past and the two finished the small flask of brandy that Teresa had stowed in her petticoat. Knowing that Ashton was just a few steps behind her, Katherine was finally able to relax and enjoy herself.

"So, which boy do you think will ask you first?" Teresa looked to Katherine in a teasing way.

"I don't care. I'm not much for picking a husband. Mum insisted that I come to this stupid thing. I would much rather stay at home with Ashton and my silly horse." Katherine gave Ashton a quick glance and continued her conversation. "I just want this night to be over, if you know what I mean." The five girls laughed, each knowing that none of them really wanted to be presented on display like prize cattle.

It was some time after the night began that Teresa mentioned casually about how dashing Ashton looked. "I know that Ashton is a servant, but have you ever noticed how truly handsome he is. I honestly don't know why I haven't noticed before, but if I had half of my wits about me, I would surely ask him to dance." Teresa and Katherine giggled shyly as they turned discreetly to him. He noticed the pair from the corner of his eye, but dismissed their girlish behavior and stared straight ahead. He had on his black and white tailored suit that Mrs. Kenningston instructed he wear and starched white gloves to match. Though much older than most of the other invited attendees of the party, his handsomeness made him stand apart from the other servants. Katherine noticed many of the young ladies peering in his direction and she soon found herself competing for his attention. Though she thought Ashton had to be aware of the immediate interests, he remained still with eyes straight ahead. After a moment, Katherine rose and addressed him, which was unusual for a lady to do at such a social event. No one seemed to mind since it was Katherine Kenningston doing it. Under any other circumstances it wouldn't be proper to speak so plainly to the servants at an event such as this, but the Kenningstons had often had the final say when it came to the matters of social etiquette.

Katherine stood before him and felt strangely shy in the presence of her longtime friend. She found herself searching for the courage to ask him for a simple favor. "Ashton, won't you go to the piano and play for our guests? It would please me so." Her voice dropped to barely a whisper. "The other girls put me up to it. I would really appreciate it if you would do this for me." Katherine gave Ashton that look that he was all too familiar with and yet could not resist.

The girls at the surrounding tables had overheard their conversation and began to join in on the request, dismissing their parents' teachings of the master-servant etiquette. "Please, just for a while? We won't bother you anymore tonight." The other servants stared at Ashton, confused with the actions of his mistress but Ashton could not refuse a wish such as this on such an important night to Katherine.

Ashton nodded, bowed elegantly, and walked smoothly to the orchestra where he apparently spoke with them about the directions of the lady whom he was escorting. Within the minute, Ashton was passionately playing the fine music that Katherine had grown to love. The room was silenced with the overpowering feelings that he displayed for the piano. Katherine once again was lost in his very presence. She pretended as if he was devoting every note to her, personally, and couldn't help but notice the jealous looks upon the other girls' faces as they swooned at the sight of him. When he finished the piece, everyone in the club clapped in response to his talent, obviously not caring that he was a mere servant of one of the richest families in the county. Katherine felt a sense of contentment in knowing that Ashton would do anything to make her smile.

After the meal, the dancing began. One by one the girls were asked to dance with the eloquently dressed local boys. Lord Wordly's son, Matthew, soon asked Katherine. Though Katherine had a distant sense of foreboding, she agreed graciously. Katherine danced under the watchful eye of Ashton and then began to feel quite uncomfortable with the young boy's advances being so open, for all to see. She often tried to excuse herself, so that she might dance with someone else, but was often interrupted by Matthew and his boyish charm. She was ultimately flattered that he was so enamored with her. They danced most of the night together and the young man soon asked Katherine out to the gardens for a stroll.

She felt as if she knew him from somewhere, but couldn't quite place him. She figured that possibly she had seen him at Sunday services on occasion. Instantly, she felt relieved that she finally knew someone outside of the manor that was pleasant enough to spend time with, not to mention someone quite so handsome. Katherine chatted aimlessly as they neared the maze of rosebushes that lined the south entrance. She felt somewhat dizzy from the brandy that she had earlier, and thought that the fresh air would do her some good. The moon was once again full and enlightened every stone path of the garden. She was enjoying herself and her company especially since she hadn't felt like socializing much this summer until now. His unusually blue eyes and attractive looks had mesmerized her as she searched for topics of interest to speak of so that they would not have to return to the party right away. She smiled to herself as she noticed the odd birthmark that was hidden on his cheek near his hairline. Such an odd shape to be on a face so perfect. As she sat soaking in his charms, she felt a change in his mood; it was as if the air around him suddenly darkened. He was staring at her with a sinister expression. It was all too soon, unfortunately, before Katherine learned of Matthew's boyish intentions.

They had found a bench to sit on near the dimly lit fountain and had been carrying on a sporadic conversation when Katherine noticed that shadowy look in Matthew's eyes. She knew at once that she shouldn't have come out into the night without a proper chaperone and soon found Matthew kissing her neck and pawing at her breast like a savage beast.

"Stop, stop at once!" She couldn't believe his manners. The memories of her terrible past came back to her in full force. He acted as though he did not hear her, his hands roving towards the bust line of her gown. She slapped him hard against the cheek and he jumped to his feet at once with his hand raised toward her.

He was instantly aware of his actions and lowered his hand acting as though he had just wanted to reach for his handkerchief. "I thought that this is what you wanted." He rubbed his cheek painfully.

She glared at him as the tears welled up in her eyes. "I should think not! I am not a simple whore. I was merely wanting to get out of that stuffy old room to enjoy some night air with you…. Maybe be better acquainted, but hardly in this fashion. Your intentions are not at all what I had expected, Mr. Wordly." Her lip was trembling with anger. Matthew took a step forward and was standing so close to Katherine that she could feel his breath on her cheek.

In almost an inaudible whisper, he spoke harshly into her ear. "Well, you hardly think that I should court you without so much as trying out your…wares?" Matthew looked at her fiercely, smiling wickedly. Katherine gasped in disbelief. Were all men only after one thing? She was angry with herself for trusting someone she had known for only a few hours. It went against everything that Ashton had instilled in her over the past few years, not to mention the promise she made to herself these past few months.

Suddenly from the path behind the marble fountain a deep voice growled, startling both of them. "Young man, or shall I say, boy, from the way you have behaved...you have greatly mistreated Miss Katherine. I suggest that you apologize to this fine lady before I remove my belt and paddle you in front of her." Ashton looked as if he were a giant in comparison to Matthew's young frame.

Matthew's face paled with shock, it seems that he had forgotten how large the manservant really was, and how protective he was rumored to be of his employer's daughter. He was clearly not in the mood to explain himself and wanted to return to the party as soon as possible, slightly embarrassed that someone had discovered how he chose to behave in front of women. It was a mistake that he vowed to himself to not make twice. He quickly turned to Katherine and bowed. "I... I apologize, my dear lady; I seem to have partaken in too much drink causing me to act entirely out of character. I didn't mean to insult you or show you any disrespect, if you'll be so kind as to accept my pardon." Before Ashton could escort him away, he turned on his heels and quickly retreated down the opposite path clearly embarrassed that his rudeness hadn't gone unnoticed.

"Ashton!" Tears were brimming in her eyes. She was unbearably embarrassed.

Ashton quickly interrupted her. "I am so very sorry, Miss Katherine, but he was acting like a brute." He regained his composure as he tried to explain his actions. "I noticed that you were absent from the hall and I—"

Katherine put her dainty gloved finger to her servant's lips. "Shh, Ashton, there is no need to explain. I'm just thankful you had come along." Still shaken from Matthew's behavior, she wrapped her arms around Ashton's giant chest. "Ashton, what would I do without you?"

He could feel her trembling from her fright. This was obviously a disturbing incident to her and he found himself placing his arms around her, allowing himself to soothe her.

"I've failed you once, my lady. I shall not let it happen again," he whispered discreetly to himself, not realizing that Katherine heard him. She could feel his muscles tighten with anger.

"Failed me...whatever do you mean?" Her eyes met his as he reluctantly explained himself.

He found himself searching for the right words. Katherine had been very sensitive lately and he didn't want to disturb her emotions further. He inhaled deeply before he spoke. "That night in the forest, I guess I can't remove that scene from my mind. I should have come sooner, if only I would have been there sooner then maybe...." Her face was so near his that he could taste her sweet breath on his lips.

Katherine pulled herself away from him, confused by his words. "Ashton, dear man, you can't possibly blame yourself for what happened that night. It was I who left the house unescorted." She stared at him stunned by his unusual show of emotions. Uncomfortable with his own words, he began to tousle her hair, pretending not to notice her looking strangely at him. "Ashton." She stepped away from him shyly, straightening her dress and beginning to smile. "I had almost forgotten, I was saving a dance for you." She gazed at him deeply with her hand outstretched for him to grasp.

Ashton stared at the hand she held in front of him, confused by her statement. "Miss Katherine, a manservant should not dance with his mistress, it isn't proper. I am certain that you are aware of that."

She approached him again and grabbed his rough work-weary hands, realizing that he was no longer wearing his gloves. "Kind sir, why have you removed your gloves?"

Ashton gave Katherine an amused look and stated clearly, "I thought that I would have to fight Mr. Wordly in order to protect your honor, fair lady. A gentleman always removes his gloves before a confrontation." He bowed overemphasizing the gesture.

"My goodness, then tonight, you are excused from your duties of being my rescuer. Let's pretend that you aren't you and I'm not me. Let's just be 'us' for just a moment." She giggled like a child, clearly amused by his behavior. "Sir Ashton, would you allow me to repay you by offering my hand in dance? I must, after all, find a way to compliment you for being so gallant." Once again, she was facing him straight on. Her sincerity made his heart ache painfully. Without another word, she placed her small, pristine hand on his cheek and guided his lips to hers. She kissed him sweetly, hotly. He allowed himself to be consumed by this gesture, but just for a moment. He then pushed himself away and gave her a perplexed look.

"I'm afraid that I don't understand, Miss Katherine." He stated breathlessly in his usual tone. Never before had a single kiss left him so confused and yet so aroused.

"Ashton, you are my best friend, and tonight you will be just that...now dance with me." She grabbed his hand and pulled him close to her body. The sweetness of her hair, the scent of her perfume, he was lost in her. They danced quietly in the moonlight; she held him as he sighed in silent surrender.

It was a few minutes till 1:00 a.m. when they finished their dance. They held each other for a moment longer. The music could no longer be heard from the distant club, but neither Katherine nor Ashton wanted this night to end so soon.

"Well, Miss Katherine Kenningston, I thank you for this kind motion as repayment for my humble attendance at this event." Ashton knew that they must rejoin the party to say their farewells before they departed for home. "Come. I'm sure the 'ever polite' Mr. Wordly is wondering about you."

Katherine laughed out loud. "I'm sure." She didn't care if she ever saw Mr. Wordly again. In fact, she had every intentions of telling her father about the way that he had addressed her this evening.

"Follow me, I guess we are both going to have to face him.

I hope I didn't muddle things too much for you." Ashton delicately led her in the direction of the club.

He led her back to her party where they said their goodbyes and were led back to the coaches. She could see Matthew at the bar, glaring at Ashton as they left the club, undoubtedly suspicious to what she and Ashton were doing in the gardens for so long. He could no doubt hear her brilliantly laugh to something that Ashton had said as the coachmen assisted them on board, which strangely gave Ashton a sense of satisfaction.

As they rode home, Katherine reached out and held his hand once again. He longed to touch her but the events of the night left him spinning. Twenty minutes into their journey, Katherine was fast asleep on Ashton's shoulder. He brushed her hair back from her serene face and felt content with just watching her breathe. When they arrived home, he carried her up the manor stairs and into her bed. He remained a moment just staring at her beauty, and then turned to leave. As he reached for the door, he heard Katherine's soft feminine voice call him. "Ashton, please…stay."

Ashton's heart ached with her words. "Miss Katherine, I cannot, you are just a confused little girl. I am not, by any means, what you want…or deserve." And he quietly shut the large wooden door, where he would remain in the hallway for a moment, breathless and in agony. It nearly killed him to deny her like this, but he knew his place and it was not supposed to be with her.

Ashton climbed down the long hidden stairwell that led to his quarters. He then poured himself a glass of red wine, loosened the top buttons of his shirt and sat at his piano. He sat and played for nearly an hour, knowing that Katherine might just be listening from somewhere amongst the large rooms far above.

Chapter Eight

MORNING CAME IN AN instant and soon Mr. and
Mrs. Kenningston were in the breakfast hall enjoying their
meal. Ashton had arisen early because of his trouble sleeping
that night and fixed a divine feast for the family.
Mr. Kenningston had already had two visits from local boys to
call upon Katherine, stating that they would like to escort her
to one place or another. She was reportedly the star of the ball,
which was no surprise to the Kenningstons. Their daughter's
pleasant affect and keen looks were sure to be an agreeable
combination in any lady. Mrs. Kenningston grinned to herself
as she remembered her own ball, so many years ago.

"It will be no time before Katie chooses a husband."
Mr. Kenningston smiled.

Shaking herself from her deep reflection of the many years
passed, she replied to her husband's statement. "Yes, I have
heard that young Matthew Wordly was quite smitten with her.
He asked if he could call upon her on Tuesday, though I don't

know if she will accept an invitation from him after the way he acted towards her." Mrs. Kenningston appeared disgusted at the thought.

Mr. Kenningston's eyes widened. "Oh, really, Lord Wordly's son? My dear, you seem to forget that we were all young once. Besides, he would be a dashing match for Katie. Blue-eyed babies all around."

Mrs. Kenningston giggled at her husband's statement. "Yes, you have a good point there, after all."

Mr. Kenningston appeared to contemplate something before speaking his next statement to his wife. "I suppose that the young Mr. Matthew does have a bit of a foul reputation, maybe he wouldn't be my first choice for my Katie, after all."

"James!" Mr. Kenningston glared at her husband. "You know as well as I do that the Wordlys are a good family; one of the finest relations from here to London. He can't possibly be as horrible as she made him out to be. We would be silly not to welcome an engagement such as that without finding out how he really is." As the Kenningstons sat contemplating their daughter's future, Ann, the kitchen maid, ran in breathless.

"S'cuse me, madam…Miss Katherine is lying in the stables violently ill. I didn't know what to do so I thought you might be of some help." The young maid looked little more than fourteen. Mrs. Kenningston rose from the table and called for Ashton.

Ashton was already by Katherine's side by the time Mr. and Mrs. Kenningston arrived. He appeared to be whispering something in Katherine's ear as they approached. Katherine's face was pale and moist from the sickness that had overtaken her and she was quite visibly ill. "Katie, my dear girl, what is the matter?" Mr. Kenningston demanded.

Ashton quickly spoke for Katherine. "She just had too much of the drink last eve. I will see her to her quarters so that she may rest at ease."

Katherine forced a smile for her parents' sake despite the

queasiness she felt at the pit of her stomach. She knew that they worried about her health lately and she wanted to avoid any unnecessary attention from the family physician, afraid that he would somehow disclose her secret. The lord and lady of the house, though significantly alarmed, had no reason to think otherwise.

Ashton gently lifted Katherine off her feet and carried her to her room. Though she was light as a feather in his bulky arms, the lesion that was not yet fully healed in his side ached painfully. He winced, but continued on, desperate to speak to Katherine before any more suspicions were raised within the house.

Ashton placed the pale Katherine safely in her bed and washed her brow with cool water from the basin nearby. His face was solemn and Katherine knew that he was troubled by something. "Ashton, what is the matter? I was merely overcome by the heat in the stables. Why wouldn't you let me tell Mum and Father that?" Katherine gave a questioning look.

"Katherine, I don't quite know how to tell you this but... I fear you are with child." He turned his face away to conceal his anger as he balled his fists. He spoke harshly through clenched teeth. "Oh, dear child, what have they done to you?"

"Ashton, if you call me a child one more time, I am going to hit you straight in the eye" The color had returned to her cheeks. "With child! Have you gone mad?" Tears were beginning to stream down her cheeks. Ashton unexpectedly turned and grabbed her securely by the shoulders, not realizing the strength that he beheld within his great hands.

His face was contorted with resentment; Katherine feared Ashton for the first time in her life. "Don't you understand, it is all my fault! I didn't save you. Now, the woman I...am supposed to take care of is with child. I couldn't save you, Katie...I couldn't save you! Don't you understand me?"

Katherine was unnerved by Ashton's erratic behavior.

"Ashton, please calm yourself. You are frightening me." She could see beads of perspiration creep down his forehead. He was obviously not well. She reached upward and felt his forehead. He was sickly hot.

"I know now what I must do." Ashton breathlessly stormed out of the room. Katherine, though still queasy, pulled on her riding boots and ran after him. "Ashton! Stop, you are not well!"

Ashton blazed into the globe room where Mr. Kenningston was trying to read the *Morning Tribune* that he had special delivered every day. Mr. Kenningston had heard the shouting from the rooms above and looked at Ashton questioningly as he strode rapidly across the marble tiled floor. With a single sweeping motion, Ashton smashed the glass door out of the large gun cabinet that stood in the corner.

"Ashton! What in bloody hell are you doing?" Mr. Kenningston jumped to his feet, spilling his coffee all over his cherry end table. The fine linen cover had soaked completely through, turning a wet brazen tan.

"I'm doing what I should have done from the very beginning." Ashton grabbed the English pistol, which he had once used to down a lame horse and tucked it into his belt. Mr. Kenningston was baffled that Ashton was not his usual calm and reserved self.

Katherine breathlessly entered the room. "Father! Please stop him, he is not well." Soon, almost the entire house staff was in to investigate the disturbance, not having ever heard Ashton raise his voice before. Before Mr. Kenningston could think to detain him, Ashton was in the stables mounting his stallion.

Katherine followed closely behind begging for him to stop. She urgently called out for him. "Ashton, please, don't do this!" Her voice had hoarsened from her pleas. She could barely see him through the dense fog that remained from the early morning. "Ashton, please!" His dark silhouette was riding away at a neck-breaking speed; the pounding of hooves fading farther and farther away. In the distance, she could see that his usually finely combed hair was once again falling about his strong face. Katherine knew at once what she must do. She had been riding since she was a girl, and had often outridden Ashton, therefore knew that could stop him before it was too late…she hoped.

Ashton did not yet know who had attacked his dear Katherine, but he was determined to find out on that day.

Katherine followed at top speed in the blinding mist. She could hear his horse running not far ahead; therefore, she knew she was gaining on him. "Ashton!" He did not answer. The moist air was making her hair heavy as it dangled over her shoulders. She could make out the stream at the end to the pasture just ahead and Ashton's horse was standing by the water's edge. "Ashton?" He was lying at the stream side panting heavily. "Ashton, please, you mustn't do this." She dismounted her horse and carefully approached him.

"Go home, Katherine!" Ashton yelled at her directly. He had never spoken to her with such a tone of voice, nor did he rise to address her as he had always done before. She was torn between utter disbelief and sheer sorrow for him. Her eyes widened as she realized that he still had the gun in his hand.

"Katie, I couldn't save you, I have failed you terribly." There was a violent look in his eyes and she could see that his cheeks were crimson with fever.

She knelt beside him. "No, Ashton. Please stop saying that. It was I who failed you. Why are you doing this? Had I have listened to your words that night, none of this would have happened. You were right, I am childish."

He then pointed the gun toward himself. She could not believe the vision before her. "Maybe I should have been the one killed that night. Anything would be better than the agony that I feel at this moment. I have broken my promise to my father to protect and care for you." Katherine knew that Ashton surely had no intentions to hurt her and she gently reached out and removed the gun from his hand. The dampness of the air had completely wetted her white riding blouse sending a chill through her body.

"Ashton, you need not prove anything, I know you have done everything in your power to protect me. It is I who is confused with your actions. Why do you treat me so when you are only paid to take care of me?" She bent down and kissed him softly. He could feel her warm salty tears mix with his.

"Katie, you don't understand... I feel more than a daring affection for you." She stared at him in disbelief. She had been in love with him since she was eight and now he has admitted to her that his admirations were ultimately the same as hers.

She kissed him again and guided his hand to her breast. "Ashton, I desire no one else but you. I am a little girl no longer and I want to share myself with you. Those men took from me something that didn't belong to them. I am offering you now what is left, if you will have me." He could control himself no longer. He rolled her onto her back and held her tightly, and kissed every inch of her beautifully sculptured face. Everything he had ever dreamed of was in his arms, finally. As he was kissing her neck and roaming to the secret places that were hidden beneath her blouse, he came to his senses and realized what he was doing. The cool, moist air had dramatically returned him to reality.

"Oh Lord, what have I done!" Ashton pushed himself away from her as she lay there breathless and in the offering for him.

"What is the matter? Please, you must understand, I love you too." Katherine gave him a mystified look.

Ashton scrambled to his feet, staring at Katherine's nearly bare breasts. "Why must you bewitch me so?" He wiped his wet forehead with his massive hands, obviously overcome by his fever.

He was clearly still angry and Katherine did not want to

enrage him any further. "It is not my intention to make you do anything that you do not want to do." She sat up, fumbling with her blouse. She fought back the tears of embarrassment as she stood to remount her horse. Ashton followed suit and mounted his horse quietly. He could not face her. He felt as if he were a betrayer to the Kenningstons, and especially to Katherine.

Afterwards, they rode in silence back to the manor, Ashton shivering with sickness. Ashton had to do some explaining for his behavior to Mr. Kenningston. It was unusual for him to lie to his employer, but until Katherine decided if she wanted the truth to be known, he thought it would be best. Mr. Kenningston believed the story about intruders stealing horses in the back pasture. Mrs. Kenningston could tell that something was happening within her household, she just couldn't quite figure out what.

Late that night while Katherine lay in her bed, thinking of the day's bizarre events, she once again heard the echoing sounds of Ashton's piano. She rose and strode across the room so that she could listen out her open window. Katherine wondered if Ashton was thinking of her at that moment. She found herself feeling concerned for him. It was as if his only way of expressing himself was in the mournful tune he was playing. He only played with this much emotion when he was deeply troubled and it was as if his music was supposed to be a secret message destined just for her.

She had to see him, speak to him. Deeply anxious to know if she had done something wrong, or had offended him somehow. Quickly she grabbed her nightgown and extinguished her lamp, hoping that the rest of the house staff had also retired. Silently, she found her way down the servant's stairwell until she was standing silently before Ashton's door. She peered through the crack in the door at him as he sat at the bench playing with his head bowed as though he were concentrating deeply. The single candle lit on the table beside

73

the piano allowed her to dimly see his face. Though cast with shadows, his expression pained her. The sorrow that loomed over him seemed to pour from his fingertips into the keys of the piano. Although the room was quite chilly, she could see his usually crisp white shirt was drenched with sweat down the middle of his back. Hair hanging in his closed eyes, it seemed almost as if he were praying. His angled jaw was tight, almost appearing as if he was in great physical pain.

She took a step closer to the door to get a better view of him and suddenly there was a loud crack from the floorboard below. Ashton stopped playing and lifted his head, sweat dripping from his tousled hair. Though he did not turn around, he knew undoubtedly who was there. His voice sounded gruff from within the dim room. "Please leave me be, Katherine. You shouldn't be down here."

Katherine remained though feeling apprehensive, and gently pushed the door open the rest of the way, stepping within the quarters. It took all of her will to muster the strength to speak so boldly to her longtime friend. "And why is that, Mr. Ashton? Am I not good enough for you? Is it beneath you to consort with the likes of me?"

Ashton spun angrily around the wooden bench, staring intensely at her. "What do you mean by that?" Once again he was claimed by the visions and sensations that lately overcame him when he saw her before him, barely clothed.

Katherine walked closer to him confused by his demeanor. "You claim you love me, but I am not good enough to share your bed?" Though that was not her intentions when she went to his door, the question did plague her mind. She untied the lace of her gown, exposing her soft breasts to him. "I know at times that you think of me as just a silly child, but admit that I have genuine feelings for you, I have always loved you, Ashton."

Ashton paused for just a moment, then rose from his seat and stood silently before her, head still sadly bowed. Slowly, his hands went to the laces in which she had just undone and he paused momentarily before he began to slowly close them back.

"Did I do something wrong?" Katherine backed away from him abruptly and turned away from him while embarrassedly tying her top laces.

"No, I did. Please leave me now. I need to be alone." Ashton stared at the floor, unable to meet her gaze. He appeared to be overwhelmed with regret and distress.

Katherine stood for a moment, staring at the man that unknowingly confused yet consumed every adolescent thought that she carried deep within her dreams. She finally had the undivided attentions of the man she secretly loved for years, and he ignored her as if she were some enamored child. Katherine did not truly understand the reasons behind his words, but she could tell when she was not wanted. She silently returned to her room where she lay awake in her bed for the better part of the night, feeling hurt yet still painfully wanting.

She found herself awakening in the morning to the soft crackling of Ashton restarting her fire. She remained still in her bed, wrought with anger and hurt from his actions the night before. She could feel Ashton walk silently across the room and tenderly touch her tousled hair. Slowly, she opened her eyes and turned to kiss his hand as it came to a rest on her cheek.

Ashton pulled his hand sharply away. "I hope all is well with you this morning, miss." Ashton stood tall, hands clasped behind his back, with all the formalities that a common butler would normally have.

"Yes, thank you." Katherine sat up at the edge of her giant bed and stretched. She decided then that if Ashton were indeed going to treat her as if she were a stranger, she would treat him just as coldly. She was a Kenningston, and people of her line of breeding didn't need to beg for anything, and she was going to keep it that way…she hoped.

Chapter Nine

AUTUMN CAME IN A flurry of invitations and Miss Katherine Kenningston had to choose wisely whom to, or not to, except to dine with. She was brimming with popularity this season and all of the local boys seemed to be quite taken with her. Although Katherine only wanted to be with Ashton, he hadn't so much as discussed the subject of what had happened by the stream side that fall morning. In fact, he had become extremely distant with her and seemed to find reasons to leave her immediate presence whenever possible. Feeling rejected, Katherine decided to once again brush aside the memory as she always did when something or someone hurt her. The baby growing inside her was more than her young mind could handle and her efforts to conceal it were becoming increasingly dim by the moment.

She had been excepting calls from Matthew Wordly more and more as of late. The week after the ball he arrived at the manor and apologized profusely in the presence of the master of the house and his wife for his actions and blamed the liquor and the moonlight for his insensitivity. Katherine kindly accepted…after all, he was Lord Wordly's son, the most esteemed man in town, next to her father. He could not possibly be as awful as he had first seemed. There seemed to be at least a formal affection growing between the two of them despite her feelings for Ashton. Mr. Wordly had called upon Miss Katherine many times at the manor and seemed quite the opposite of the man she had originally acquainted herself with.

It was mid-October and Ashton was out clearing the pumpkin patch when Katherine approached him in a somewhat formal manner. "Mr. Ashton, I must inform you that I find myself strangely compelled to speak with you about a matter of distinct importance, despite our indifference as of late." She lowered her voice so that only he could hear her. "Though I realize that since you have had your way with me as you apparently wanted and haven't spoken nearly a sentence to me since, I still feel obligated to tell you that Mr. Wordly is going to ask father for my hand in marriage."

Ashton stood and straightened his housecoat. The top three buttons of his shirt were undone, exposing a dark tuft of perspiration-moistened hair. Noticing the direction of her gaze, he quickly did them up, it was clear that her desire for him was still present somewhere within her. Katherine felt a pang of sadness in her heart for his actions. Was this not the man who had professed his love for her two months ago and then displayed it not in his actions? He continued to pull at the withered vines, not even turning towards her as he addressed her so harshly.

"What is to be, will be…miss." His words were stone. She saw his eyes glance to her swollen belly and pulled her shawl tightly around the front. Tears began to stream down her reddened cheeks. It was not enough to be embarrassed by her situation alone, and she now felt that even her dear friend had denied her his companionship because of it.

"What ever happened to my dear Ashton who would do anything for my happiness? You once laid your life down for me, why am I now so easily dismissed?" She could see fury growing in his eyes, but he remained distant for the moment. She turned and began to leave the garden, madly wiping her eyes.

"Katie," he spoke gently and she turned to meet his gaze, "it is because you are not so easily dismissed that I treat you as I do. You and I are from different worlds, I am not meant for you. Go now to your Mr. Wordly. He can provide for you, as I undoubtedly cannot." He removed his gloves, showing her his work-weary blistered hands, his voice harshened as he tried to make her understand the reality of his situation. "I am your manservant, and as I need not remind you, it is just a mere step above a stable boy. I am paid to care for you, surely you understand this? Do you really think that we could be together?" He paused for a moment to restrain his rising temper. "What could I possible give you in comparison to your Mr. Wordly?" He shook his head sadly, breathing deeply before he resumed. "Would you really rid yourself of your fineries to join me in dusting the china? I should think not, nor would I allow it. I made a terrible mistake last summer; I put my heart before yours, and that was wrong. Though you were right about my lonely existence here at the manor, I had no right as a servant to cross the boundaries that are set forth for my kind. I am here to serve you and your family, and that is all I must do."

"But I love you. Does that mean nothing to you at all?" Katherine pleaded with him openly.

He brushed back his glistening hair and sighed. From somewhere inside he realized that even his father's death had not brought him so much pain. "My love will not put bread on the table. You need to speak with your parents tonight about the child. If you are to accept Matthew's hand in marriage, you will need their help in this matter. I can be of no more use to you. I love you, Katie, but you must, for all of our sakes, forget about me." His voice was beginning to shake. "Good day, miss." He bowed formally and abruptly turned his back to her in efforts to conceal his emotions.

Katherine ran to the manor sobbing. Her mother and father were soon at her side, arms around her, inquiring about what was the matter. She decided to finally tell them in great detail the events of the summer.

After calling her parents into the parlor, Katherine mustered the courage to speak about everything. "Mum, Father, I have to tell you something of importance. Last summer when I was attacked, I... I was also wronged by those men. I was ashamed to tell you. If it weren't for Mr. Ashton, I would have surely been killed." She stopped for a moment and then broke the news of the child. "I know that you had grand dreams of me marrying a gentleman, but I cannot possible enter in an engagement with this child. You must understand." Her loving parents listened silently, horrified. They will never again look at her as a young girl. She has been bearing the stresses of womanhood before their very eyes and they hadn't even noticed. After great discussion of the season's tragedies, they were finally able to get over the shock of the news. The problem was now, what to do with the baby, and how to seek revenge on the men that ruined their little girl. All three agreed they couldn't possibly mention a thing to Mr. Wordly for he surely would not want her to be his wife. A man of his status could easily choose from any of the other prized young girls that were offered.

After a long display of emotions and sorrow that they felt for their young daughter, they knew they needed to openly discuss the unborn child. "We could send you away for 'lessons' until you have the child and then you could return with an orphaned cousin." Mr. Kenningston felt that it was best to tell his daughter something to ease her mind until they figured out precisely what to do. He and his wife both knew that this was not going to be the plan. Having the child raised in even the same township would be a danger to their honor, what if the secret got out? Katherine was pleased that they had not mentioned giving the child to the local convent to raise as it was common in these times to do so when an unwanted child is born.

After nearly an hour of discussing the details that were involved, Katherine finally felt some relief. "That is a splendid idea, Father, we will tell Matthew tonight." She seemed positively overjoyed with this story and her eyes lightened with happiness. She ran to her dressing room to prepare for his arrival, trying desperately not to think about her and Ashton's discussion earlier.

While she was dressing herself, Ashton glimpsed a view of her through her bedroom window. He had been out locking the stables as he had every night since the attack, unsure whether it was to keep the thieves away or to prevent any further temptation from Katherine. There would be no second time that he would allow the woman he so desperately loved to be harmed.

Katherine was primping before the mirror, awaiting the familiar sound of coaches coming up the roadway. He stared upward to the second-floor window wondering if she was thinking about him as he was her. Though she was as beautiful as and angel, Ashton knew that Matthew would never see or understand her true beauty. He had recently heard rumors in town about Matthew's appetite for beautiful women, as well as his fondness of the drink. This was a terrible combination for someone with so short a temper.

Matthew arrived in all of his usual splendor; his coach was known to be the finest in town. He entered the doorway of the grand house and gave a respectful bow to Miss Katherine. "Good evening, my lady, I have brought you some flowers from the town's shops. I thought that they would suit you nicely."

His eyes met hers and she once again felt a sense of knowing him from somewhere before, somewhere before the ball. She retrieved the large bouquet and turned respectfully to him. "How very gracious of you, Mr. Wordly."

Mrs. Kenningston and Katherine curtseyed officially.

Mr. Wordly smiled. "Matthew, from now on. Please, I insist." He bowed respectfully back winking at her slyly.

"Matthew it is. Come now our supper awaits." Mrs. Kenningston invited him in to the main hall. Katherine seemed to cower in his presence with shyness. She quickly beckoned him into the fine dining room away from Ashton's intolerable gaze. He stood coldly at the doorway as Matthew entered the dining room not bowing or acknowledging his exit as the other servants had. Katherine thought to herself about how strange Ashton's behavior was when but hours earlier he was all but demanding that she marry Matthew.

They had barely sat in their designated chairs when Matthew began speaking. "Mr. Kenningston," Matthew addressed him nervously. Katherine was positively giddy with excitement. "Before we begin enjoying this fine meal, I feel that there is a need to discuss something of importance with you tonight."

Ashton and the kitchen maids were now beginning to serve the lamb, moving slowly as if to hear more of the conversation. The two maids serving the food looked sympathetically toward Ashton, feeling from across the room a strange air of sorrow come over him. Though they did not know the extent of Ashton's relationship with Katherine, they knew that they had somehow become closer than they had ever been, until recently. It seemed that the room had suddenly gone completely silent. All attentions were focused on Matthew's announcement. "I will be going away to the university tomorrow, but I want to assure that my dear Katherine will be here for me when I return." He winked at Katherine.

Katherine's goblet slipped from her fingers and spilled its contents on the tablecloth before her. "Oh dear, Katherine, are you all right?" Mrs. Kenningston questioned her daughter, sensing the intensity of the moment. She felt certain that Matthew was going to know that there was something going on.

"Yes, Mother, I'm fine. Matthew, do go on." Katherine smiled beautifully. Ashton arrived at her side and was soon wiping the tablecloth meticulously, as if to remain in the room a moment longer with Katherine.

Matthew looked to Mr. and Mrs. Kenningston then continued, "As, I was saying...I will be at the university until April and when I return, it would be my honor to..." He suddenly began to stammer. "What I am trying to say is that I would like to have Miss Katherine's hand in marriage, but only if we were to have your blessing of course." Though his false smile had no effect on Ashton, Mr. Kenningston seemed taken with his charm.

Katherine's eyes widened. Mrs. Kenningston sighed in relief. They would not have to send their dear daughter away for the duration of her pregnancy. She could remain at the house while Matthew was away and have plenty of time remaining to explain a sudden appearance of a child. Katherine found herself comforted and relieved at the thought of remaining at the manor for a while longer.

Mr. Kenningston wiped his mouth and smiled. "Why of course, son." It was as if a great weight had been lifted from the Kenningston family. Katherine's marriage prospect would be conveniently out of the way during the crucial months of her pregnancy.

Ashton served the wine and pastries all the while feeling blessed that he would have a few precious months left with

Katherine before the wedding. He desired nothing more than to be present for her during her pregnancy. It was only right that he help her in any way he could since he felt somewhat responsible for the mishap. The meal carried on with Mrs. Kenningston and Katherine chatting away aimlessly at wedding plans. Matthew and Mr. Kenningston finally retired to the globe room for some brandy and cigars.

"Ashton, dear man," Mr. Kenningston had apparently begun to feel his brandy, "come join us for some spirits! Sit down...you know," he jabbed hard at Matthew with his elbow, "you would think that this man and my dear Katie are brother and sister the way they carry on. They rarely ever leave each other's sight!" Though Mr. Kenningston was a very intelligent man when it came to politics and investments, he was totally unaware of his daughter's admiration for her servant.

Matthew scowled at Ashton as he lit his cigar. "I know, I recall our first meeting in the gardens at the ball." Ashton grinned to himself also remembering their first encounter. He relished the memory of Matthew's horrified face when he had confronted him that night after he discovered his adamant disrespect for his mistress.

"Well, you won't be needing to bother my Katie anymore after these next few months, now will you," Matthew stated. The tension was openly mounting between them.

Even Mr. Kenningston appeared to be taken aback by their behavior. "Oh, come now, my Katie will find time for both of you, so you two had best just learn to agree upon some kind of arrangement. We're all going to be just like family!" Mr. Kenningston chuckled nervously finding the interaction between the two bizarre.

"Katie is a treasure that I care not to share." Matthew blew smoke out slowly, grinning coolly at Ashton. He then took another sip of his brandy and dismissingly waved his hand towards the door. "You are excused now, Mr. Ashton, Mr. Kenningston and I have some business matters to discuss."

Ashton, finding certain aspects of the company of the room detestable, compliantly rose to leave, calmly reciprocating Matthew's hateful glare. "If that will be all, I bid you good night, sirs," he said sarcastically as he shut the door quietly behind him.

As Ashton was returning to the dining room, he wanted nothing better than to tell Katherine what a mistake she was making; he wanted to profess his undying affections to her and plead with her not to marry that brute. After a moment of reflection, he knew though that he must lay his emotions to rest, it was something he must learn to live with. Marrying Matthew would be the best thing for Katherine and he knew it. He glanced at her woefully while she finished her coffee. Such beauty could never be wasted in his presence. He was but a servant, a poor man that would never mean anything to a woman of her status. Though he felt at this time sorrow for his future loss, he could not help but to notice Katherine's astonishing presence. He cherished her every breath and he was instantly overcome with the memories that he had of her and him alone. The delicate fragrance of her hair returned to him as if a reality. Just to watch her merely exist was enough to halt all of the armies in London.

Katherine soon realized that Ashton was staring at her strangely. Once again their eyes and hearts were connected and she was unable to conceal her attentions. She wanted to run up to him and tell him that she wanted no one else but him and that she could not possibly live without seeing his warm face every day. She mouthed the words 'I'm sorry' and he knew that deep within this was true. They were as if in a stupor when Mrs. Kenningston awoke Katherine with a tap on the shoulder. "Katherine, dear child, what is it? You look as though you've lost your wits!"

"What? Oh nothing, I was just dreaming I guess." Katherine spoke loud enough for Ashton to hear. "Mr. Ashton, I will be retiring after I see our guest off, will you be kind enough to draw me a hot bath?" Matthew had just returned from the globe room with Mr. Kenningston and overheard the request of Katherine to her servant. He looked as though he were about to have a fit of anger as he thought of Ashton spending another moment alone with Katherine.

"Yes, milady." His eyes met Matthew's while bowing gallantly to her. Ashton knew that he must savor every second with her because they would soon be lost to the esteemed Mr. Wordly. Katherine and the Kenningstons bid Matthew a good night and he was soon exiting the manor to his coach.

Ashton had filled her bath with gardenia-perfumed water and rose oil. He laid out her favorite nightclothes and proceeded to light the candles and stir the coals in the fireplace. The dark skies threatened snow and Katherine's bedroom was often drafty. As he placed the logs on the fire he heard Katherine enter the room.

"Thank you, Ashton." Her voice was nearly a whisper. Pretending not to notice, he continued to stoke what was the now roaring blaze. He felt her approach and stand dangerously near him but could not find the strength to distance himself. He needed to continue to act impartial to her, but even a man as strong as he was, found it difficult to restrain himself. This morning's display of emotions was not something he was proud of, in fact, he felt slightly embarrassed by his actions. Unflinchingly, he walked away from her and placed her bath mat before the giant porcelain tub. Katherine began to remove her clothes anonymously in silence, struggling with the waistline. Her ever-expanding abdomen was more than her fancy gowns could handle. Ashton saw her difficulties and began to help her.

"I see we must take out some of the waists of these dresses," he stated, still trying to remain indifferent. He tugged at the sash and instantly the dress fell to the floor.

"Yes, I know." Her voice quivered familiarly and he looked

85

up at her. He saw her wince and at once began to sob. His heart
sank regretfully at the sight of her feeling so distressed.

"Katherine, are you not feeling well?" He tried to put up an
emotionless front as he carefully returned the dress to the
armoire.

"Look at me. I look like a swollen cow! How could such a
man find me attractive when I look positively appalling."
Ashton felt overwhelming pity for Katherine and reluctantly
put his arms around her naked body, trying to calm her.

"Shh, Katherine, it's all right. It is only a temporary state.
Besides, I still think you are beautiful." She hugged him
lovingly in return. He stroked her naked back with his large
calloused hands. He then picked her up effortlessly and placed
her in the tub. The fire was burning and casting faint shadows
along the walls of the room. He wet her long hair and washed
it gently. He reflected on how strange it was that just a year ago
he would have thought nothing of washing her hair and yet
now he found it strangely sensual. Though he concentrated on
his duties of the following day to remove the unwanted
thoughts of her from his mind, he realized the importance of his
closeness to her. His every motion soothed her. He could feel
that she was relaxing and feeling increasingly more at ease
with his touch.

After a moment of this silent interaction, Katherine spoke
softly to him. "Ashton, why can't things be as they were, we
were such great friends. Now you hardly speak to me." Her
voice softened as the tears began to fall. "I know that you think
of me as just a silly girl, but I need you. I can't do this alone."
He rinsed her hair one last time and she turned to face him. He
thought it was best that he not answer her for fear of exposing
his true feelings once again, he felt strangely embarrassed by
his words from earlier that day. A man of his age had no right
to act so found of a woman this young. Especially a man with
no money or entitlements to offer her.

Her eyes danced beautifully in the firelight. She then rose

and he toweled her delicate skin dry. Quickly, he assisted her into her sleeping clothes and escorted her to the oversized canopy bed. As he covered her with the embroidered coverlet, she spoke to him reminiscently. "Do you remember lying in this very bed last summer nearly dead?"

She turned to him once again and he remembered the events that led to the large scar on his back. "Yes, I do. You sat with me every day until I was healed." He brushed back her hair gently. "I never thanked you."

"I tell you now that as you lay there naked, beneath my sheets, it was the first time that I had ever longed to touch a man. As I touched your lips, I wondered what it would be like to kiss them. I know now that it was silly for a girl like me to ever think to gain the affections of a man such as yourself."

Ashton noticed a strange look in her eyes as she continued to speak but found himself curiously interested in their destination.

"I must admit I am not remorseful for what we did by the stream that day." Moving closer to him, he could feel that her breathing had deepened. She slowly began to unbutton his starched collar.

"Katherine, please, you don't understand how difficult it is to resist you. I am merely a man, after all." He tried to stand but she fiercely pulled him onto the bed. "Miss Katherine, it is important that you listen to me, you are just a bit overemotional right now. A woman goes through changes when she is with child, I assure you that this type of affections toward me is not valid."

She had almost completely unbuttoned his shirt and was kissing her way down his chest. "Ashton, I am a woman now, as you know. Do you not feel the same toward me?" She had his belt completely undone and was kissing the patch of hair beneath. She could feel him breathing heavily also.

"Katherine, don't. You don't know what you are doing to me. Please stop. This just isn't right. You are betrothed to

Mr. Matthew." Ashton found himself unable to resist her advances any further.

She could feel his hands slowly stroking the hair at the back of her head. "You are my dearest friend Ashton, please, I need you."

His penis was completely exposed now, fully erect. She licked at it hungrily as he groaned in delight. Her hands stroked his chest as she suckled his manhood. After a few moments she rose to kiss him. He felt warmness as she straddled him moving rhythmically on the bed. Beads of sweat formed on her forehead as she began to move at a quicker pace. He cupped her breasts as she began to whimper. She rode him for a few moments longer as he felt her muscles tighten and then come to a rest. She lay atop his chest breathless still kissing him while he finished almost simultaneously.

Chapter Ten

IT WAS FIVE DAYS before Christmas at the Kenningston manor and the skies were darkening to what would be the worst snowstorm in years. The snowflakes shone like diamonds outside the large window at the entrance as the lights from the house reflected off each and every one. Ashton was noisily dragging the twelve-foot Christmas tree into the main hall. The icy cold made it a difficult task but he knew that Katherine had always loved to decorate the tree. Though she was engaged to Mr. Wordly, Ashton found himself hopelessly attached to Katherine, treating her as if he himself were marrying her. He found himself thinking of the child within her as if it were his own. Ultimately it was difficult for him to distinguish that things were any different since he was the only companion that she had at this point. Mr. and Mrs. Kenningston asked Katherine not to venture into town afraid that their secret would be made known.

As soon as the ice was melted from the tree's lavish bows,

Ashton helped Katherine hang the fragile, timeless ornaments. They were joyously singing Christmas carols as the fire blazed in the main fireplace, secretly kissing each other as only lovers would do. Both ultimately afraid that Mr. or Mrs. Kenningston would somehow discover them and their clandestine relationship. If the secret affair were to be discovered, Ashton might possibly be cast out of the manor forever. Katherine's belly was now visible beneath her dress and all of the household staff was paid duly for their secrecy. It seemed that Ashton and Katherine's love for each other was not the only thing being kept a secret at the manor.

Katherine giggled like a child as she attempted to hang a sleeping cherub on a far above branch. "I love Christmas. It reminds me of when I was a child. Things were much more simple then. I remember that you used to scold me for eating all the candy canes before the tree was even trimmed." She breathed deeply, obviously contemplating something. "Ashton, will you hang the star for us this year?"

Mrs. Kenningston entered the room and smiled at the pleasant interaction between the two. She knew that Katherine needed Ashton's support and friendship since she was not as close to her daughter as he. Though there was already over three feet of new fallen snow on the ground outside the manor the large room was warm and pleasant. "I think that this year's tree is the best ever." Mrs. Kenningston smiled.

The tree's topper was sent from Katherine's great aunt from Norway and it was always an honor to be chosen to place it on the utmost boughs. As Ashton finished hanging the star, Katherine tripped on the tree's pedestal and Ashton caught her with his strong arms. "Like an angel from the heavens, she fell unto me," Ashton sang jokingly.

She inhaled his pine and spice scent deeply. "Thank you, Sir Ashton. I guess I'm beginning to be a bit unbalanced these days." He gazed deeply into her eyes. Mrs. Kenningston cleared her throat loudly as she left the room to retrieve a few finishing touches for the tree. They laughed simultaneously as the sleeping cherub slipped from its perch and landed safely on one of the lower branches.

"Yes, Miss Katherine, I see that." Ashton glanced downward to her abdomen.

She punched him in the arm jokingly and turned to warm herself in front of the fire, contemplating what gift would make her servant happy. "Ashton, what would you like for Christmas? Whatever you want, I shall get it for you." Her eyes twinkled in the firelight.

"Miss Katherine, do not concern yourself with my needs, you have much more to worry about this holiday season. What is it that you fancy this year?" He let go of her waist.

"I have no preference this year. Mum always gets me slippers and perfumes. Remember that awful pair of dog skin slippers from last year." She could barely contain her laughter.

Ashton chuckled loudly. "Yes, I believe it wasn't such a tragedy that they made their way too close to the firestones last spring. You had better sit for a moment or two, you look positively flushed, my lady." He guided her to a nearby settee. "Let me fetch you a cup of tea to calm you." The wind began to howl outside and the falling snow made it impossible to see ten feet out of the window.

He soon returned with a warm cup of chamomile tea and honey. She sipped quietly as she gazed into the warm fire. "What is it, dear Katherine, you look so forlorn." Ashton turned to finished with the last details of the tree, quickly arranging the gifts that they had recently received neatly beneath it.

"Oh, nothing, just feeling a bit emotional these days I guess." He then walked over to the fire to place another log where he heard her whisper, "Why couldn't we just run away? It is you that I love, can't you see that?" Katherine hadn't meant for Ashton to hear her statement but, sadly, he had. He continued to stoke the fireplace as the sound of a tree cracking under the weight of the snow sounded in the distance. His heart ached. He wanted nothing more but to grant her wishes but knew that it wouldn't be the right thing for to do, for her sake. She needed someone to care for her in the luxury that she deserved and expected and he could not provide that.

Hoping to ease her saddened heart he thought it best that she return to her quarters for some much needed rest. "Are you ready to retire?" He approached her and pretended not to notice the tear streaming down her cheek.

She quickly wiped her face with her lace sleeve and grabbed a hold of his arm. "Yes, I guess I should, I have been so tired these days." He guided her up to her bedroom, helped her to bed and bowed good night. She gave him that sleepy welcoming look again but he difficultly closed the door. As he descended the stairs to his quarters, he thought of his holiday wishes. He wanted her for Christmas, plain and simple.

When Katherine was safely in bed, Ashton went to the stables and readied his horse ready to carry out his plan. The freezing temperatures made his fingers numb and slow, but he eventually was able to mount her and head down the roadway to town to buy her the gift that he had been thinking of for weeks. The path was nearly invisible with the drifts that accumulated over the past few hours. Ashton clumsily pulled his overcoat closed as the icy wind cut to his skin.

Though his mind told him that it was dangerous to be out at this time of night, his heart led him onward. After nearly an hour, Ashton saw the first lamplight flickering in the distant town. He reached into his overcoat and felt for the familiar weight of his father's gold pocket watch, which in less than half of an hour would be trade stock for a locket and chain for Katherine. He couldn't afford to get her fancy rabbit lined gloves, or perfumes, or any of the other fineries which she already had, but it was important for him to give her something to remember him by, something from his heart.

PRESENTLY UNTITLED

After what seemed like an eternity of riding through the treacherous snow, he saw the main entrance road that led into the town. There were few lights burning this time of night and he only hoped that someone would be available to help him with his wares. He banged on the door of the Old Town Shoppe. The familiar face of Johan, the shopkeeper, peered through the frost glazed window. "Ashton, what are you doing out this time of night, and in this kind of weather!" Johan guided Ashton into the shop, clumsily lighting candles along the way.

"I wanted to get something for Katherine. She is recently engaged to Lord Wordly's son, and I believe that this will be the last season that I will be in her service. I saw a gold locket and chain that I thought she might fancy, if you still have it." The old shopkeeper at once walked to the back of the store and opened the glass showcase, removing the delicate necklace. He looked at Ashton questioningly and asked if it was the locket that he was inquiring about.

"Yes, that is the one. I don't have any money but I thought you might be interested in my late father's pocket watch." He held out the ornately carved gold pocket watch and the shopkeeper inspected it.

After a moment of looking at the watch, he handed it back to cold-weary servant. "Ashton, my dear man, I'm afraid that it just wouldn't be right for me to take this as a trade. This watch must be worth ten times that locket, I would be stealing if I were to accept this as payment." He stared at Ashton puzzled.

"Please, I have no use for it. I can't tell you how important it is that you accept." Ashton flashed him a convincing smile. "I have no need for such things."

The old man saw a desperation that he had never seen in a man before. The man thought of a way to cover his pity for Ashton, he had known Ashton for many years just as he had know his father before him. He did not feel comfortable doing

93

a transaction where Ashton got the shortest end of the stick but knew that it must be important if he was out on a night like this. "OK, but only if you take one of those boxes of Swiss chocolate with you."

Ashton smiled. "It's a deal then." The shopkeeper wrapped the items with brightly colored paper and bows and Ashton went out once again into the snowy night.

As Ashton began to carefully place the chocolate in his horse's saddlebags and the locket in his breast pocket, a sharp pain seared in his back and he screamed in agony. The stab wound to his kidney during the summer hadn't healed as it should have and he was beginning to have complications as time wore on. Ashton called out but the depth of the falling powdered snow muffled his scream. After a few minutes, while trying to regain his strength, he was able to weakly mount his horse once again and begin his long journey home.

Somewhere midway on his journey, the pain hit him once again, more intense than ever, and he lost consciousness. Fortunately his arms fell around the horse's neck so he did not plummet to the icy ground below. The sub-zero temperatures would mean sure death for anyone caught in the elements for any length of time.

Katherine awoke chilled in the dead of night to find that her fire had gone out. "Ashton? Could you bring some wood for the fire? It has almost gone completely out." It was unusual for Ashton not to keep the fire blazing in the hearth for fear that Katherine might experience any sort of discomfort. Though Ashton didn't know it, she was all too aware that he had once again begun sleeping outside her bedroom door in his servant's chair. His overprotectiveness had only been amplified with her pregnancy. "Ashton?" She arose from her bed and discovered that Ashton was not at his usual post. She pulled on her house robe and slippers and quickly descended the stairs to the servant's quarters. She was alarmed to find that Ashton was not in his room.

She crossed the hall and tapped lightly on Ann, the laundry maid's door. "Yes?" Ann sleepily peered through the slit in the doorway.

"Have you seen Mr. Ashton?" Katherine couldn't explain it but she had a terrible sense that something was wrong.

"Last I saw of him, he was in the stables tending to his horse. But I wouldn't worry, he knows better than to go out on a night like this." Ann yawned loudly.

"Thank you." Katherine's heart sank. She quickly pulled on her boots, white rabbit-skin coat, and mittens and headed for the stables. Realizing that Ashton's horse was nowhere in sight, she saddled Tom and threw a few spare horse blankets over the back of him. Soon she was heading down the nearly hidden pathway. Her breath was like white mist as she maneuvered her way down the snowy forest path. Her face was stinging with the cold. She knew that if Ashton was in any kind of danger and was to survive, she must find him quickly. Her horse dredged slowly along the snowdrifts, some nearly waist high. She patted her ivory stallion's neck praying that he move swiftly along. "Come on, Tom, you can do it, old boy." Her lips were so cold that her words slurred.

She continued on for quite a while, searching every dark corner for a sign of Ashton. She felt the baby kick on occasion, as if telling her to turn back. Deep inside, Katherine knew the dangers of being out at this time of night, especially in the dead of winter, but still she droned on. After riding for half an hour she began to think that it was imperative that she turn back. Ashton had probably realized that the weather was treacherous and stayed at the inn downtown.

It was during a break in the clouds that the moon shone on a figure blocking the trail ahead. Her heart jumped in fear when she sensed movement ahead. She was nearly in a full panic when she recognized the familiar coal black face of Ashton's stallion. It was then that she saw a dark shape slumped over the horse's neck, realizing that it was the still body of her closest friend and her heart dropped in agony.

"Ashton!" She jumped from her horse and waded through the ice-cold snow. She knew at once that he was in distress when she saw his pale face. She grabbed the wool horse blankets from Tom and placed them around Ashton's lifeless body. Vigorously, she rubbed his hands and face, hoping to transfer some of her warmth to his body. Katherine then hastily led his weary stallion back to the path home.

When Katherine arrived at the manor, she awoke the house staff and instructed them to draw a hot bath for Ashton immediately. There wasn't any sign of life from him by this time and she began to fear that she was too late. Mr. and Mrs. Kenningston soon followed the rest of the household, frantic and inquiring if there had been an attack on the manor. They had heard the commotion from their bedrooms and were alarmed when they saw Ashton being carried in by the stable boys.

The house staff soon had Ashton placed in the warm bath and he was beginning to awaken. His shallow breaths were evening out and his eyes opened cautiously. He was obviously confused when he discovered that he was submerged in a bathtub in nothing but his underclothes, staring languidly at his onlookers.

Katherine tenderly kissed his forehead. "Ashton, what in heavens were you doing out in this weather?" Katherine scolded.

Ashton sleepily turned his head and tried to focus on Katherine. "I wanted to get you something." He motioned to his overcoat. He lifted his arm as if it weighed a ton.

Katherine peered over her shoulder confused. "He must be delirious. Ann, fetch some more hot water." Curious, she rose to investigate, somewhat apprehensive to what she might find.

She was reaching into his front pocket when her parents cautiously entered the room. "Is Mr. Ashton alive?" They seemed somewhat alarmed when they saw his half-undressed pale body in the bathtub.

"Yes, but barely, it seems that he had gone to town to get me…this." She held up the richly wrapped gift for them to see. "I don't know what could possibly be so important that he venture out on a night like this." Strangely overcome by the night's excitement she found herself announcing her feelings toward her servant without even realizing what she had done. "I don't know how to explain this to you, but we have fallen in love. I don't know when it happened or why, but there is nothing that you can do to change this."

Mrs. Kenningston gasped. She had suspicions these past few months that her daughter had growing emotions for Ashton, but thought that her engagement with Mr. Wordly was enough to distract her.

Katherine was soon kneeling again beside the bathtub sponging Ashton off with the warm water. "Katherine, I think that you should let the servants care for him, you need your rest." Katherine ignored her mother and continued to care for her servant attentively.

After a moment, feeling remorseful for her proclamation, Katherine excused her parents from the room, knowing that they were disappointed with her. "Mother, go back to bed. I will retire as soon as I know that Ashton is safe." Mrs. Kenningston retreated to her room, for the first time, fully aware of her daughter's concern and feelings for her manservant.

Once Ashton's color had returned to normal, Katherine had Ann help her dress him into some warm woolen bedclothes that she had borrowed from her father and placed him into bed. "I am having Ann prepare some of her chamomile and lavender butter to rub your back with." She removed his shirt once he was partially covered with the blankets, trying to retain as much warmth as possible.

Ann soon returned with her warmed herbal remedy for exposure. Katherine began to massage Ashton's weary muscles with the aromatic oils. "Ashton, I don't understand why you would brave the worst storm of the year to buy me a gift. Besides, how could you possibly afford it?" She was immediately embarrassed for her statement. Ashton had once told the Kenningstons that he sent all of his earnings to a disabled cousin in London, but Katherine discovered a few years ago, purely by accident, that he was giving all of his pay anonymously to a poor family down the road. Katherine was soon rubbing Ashton's back gently to bring the circulation back to his skin.

She was deep in thought when she heard Ashton say, in almost a whisper, "I love you too." Before Katherine could reply, she heard him give a loud snore. Ashton had fallen immediately into a deep sleep.

Katherine quietly picked up the gift and blew out the lamps in Ashton's room. She found her way threw the dimly lit house to the large twinkling Christmas tree. She placed the small package beneath the tree, still wondering what could have been so important for him to travel out in these bitter temperatures to get. She remained for a moment, basking in the glory of the giant, shimmering tree. This would be her last Christmas at the manor, so she was going to make it the best holiday ever.

Christmas Eve came with no reprieve from the weather. Although they would not have the usual guests for dinner this year due to the stormy conditions, Katherine was glowing with excitement. Mr. Kenningston had decided, unknowingly similar to his daughter's summer bash, that he would invite the house staff to join them this year for dinner. All but an important few were excused to be with their families, so the remaining might as well have a celebration also. This evening there were no boundaries, no social inconveniences, just people enjoying each other's company on a traditional holiday at home. Six bottles of the finest champagne were uncorked by nine o'clock, and even Ashton was indulging in a bit of the spirits. He was later seen excitedly dancing about the hall with Katherine reminiscent of a schoolboy in love. Mrs. Kenningston whom had helped herself with quite possibly a few drinks too many herself was singing glorious carols with the better part of the house staff. Katherine enjoyed seeing everyone so happy. She danced with Ashton, her father, and anyone else that asked while the others took turns playing festive tunes on the grand piano. Her ankles were soon tired and she sat to enjoy a cup of hot chocolate.

Soon Mr. Kenningston announced that it was time to open the gifts. It was tradition for the Kenningstons to open one of their gifts on Christmas Eve. The Kenningstons, knowing that the house staff would be their only guests this year, had secretly purchased gifts that uniquely fit each servant, as well as a bit of money to fill their stockings with. Ole' St. Nick was very gracious this year. Each servant opened his or her gift eagerly; the Kenningstons were known for their kindheartedness when it came to the servants. Janice got a new pair of woolen gloves that she desperately needed. The Kenningstons had also included a pair for each of her children and a large brick of chocolate for every one of them. Ann, the maid, got a powder blue quilt woven of the finest fleece, one that she was seen spying through a shop window last fall. She was nearly in tears when she held it high for all to see, she had not gotten a gift in which she had cherished as much, since her parents were alive.

Finally, it was Katherine's turn. The room was silenced in anticipation as she decided to open the gift that Ashton had bought for her. Her hands trembled as she carefully unwrapped the paper, revealing a small box. She opened the velvet-lined box and was awestruck as she admired the brilliant gold locket inside. She was amazed by its beauty. All eyes were on Katherine and her precious gift. She stared at Ashton with amazement because she knew that this gift was far beyond his means and finances. She deeply wanted to once again inquire how he was able to afford a gift such as this, but knew he would never admit to her that he couldn't afford it.

Feeling uncomfortable with everyone focusing their attention on them, he spoke. "It is so that you can carry a lock of the baby's hair with you after he, or she, is born. Let me put it on you to see how it looks." Ashton gently lifted her hair and placed the gold chain around her. He wanted very much at that moment to kiss the back of her neck, to caress her once again. He loved her more at that moment then he had ever loved anyone before and everyone at the party could feel it.

Mr. and Mrs. Kenningston then gave each other a look, each knowing what the other was thinking. It unfortunately would soon be time to act. They would not have their only daughter give up an engagement to an esteemed man such as Mr. Wordly to run off with a butler, despite the fondness they felt for him.

It was a few hours after midnight when Katherine decided to send everybody to their respective quarters. "Come now, everyone, you really must go to bed or it will be only your heads singing in the morning." There was an agreeing laughter throughout the hall. Mr. and Mrs. Kenningston headed for the grand stairway, arm in arm, looking especially cheerful. Katherine held Ashton tightly about the arm and guided him toward the servant's stairwell. "Ashton, I think you should retire also."

He grabbed her by her pluming waistline and pulled her toward him, passionately. "You think so, my dear lady?" His breathing was heavy now. He grinned attractively at her.

"Yes, Mr. Ashton. You have had more to drink than I think you can handle, under these circumstances." The locket around her neck shone in the lamplight. Katherine led Ashton to the tiny room that he slept in. She lit a candle and placed it on the small piano that stood in the far corner. She closed the door behind her after she entered the room as Ashton began to ramble.

Clearly drunk, she ignored most of what he was saying, knowing that he would be embarrassed tomorrow. "We could be married, you and I. If only I were born titled as you were. Being that I am presently 'untitled,' I guess that it will never happen, not truly anyway. Silly me to think such things could happen to me. You asked me once if I was ever in love and the answer is yes, I was in love once before." He yawned loudly. "She was in college with me. She stayed with me throughout my studies at the university. Though we never entered into an arrangement, her and I had an understanding that we would be engaged when I had completed my studies. She left me when I came here to work; she couldn't bear to be in association with a mere 'butler.' I don't blame her though, after all, what do I have to offer." He looked lovingly at Katherine. "She didn't treat me as you do. You treat me as though I were the greatest man in the world. You make me feel loved. We could have been married, if only..."

He stumbled over the end table and a vase came crashing down. She undressed him, placed him in the bed and he was soon fast asleep. She placed her head on the pillow next to him, pondering his drunken statements, and before she knew it, she too was fast asleep.

Chapter Eleven

THE WINTER DRONED ON and Ashton and Katherine spent the rest of it just enjoying each other's company. They were once again the close friends that they once were. Ashton would be seen frantically riding in the middle of the night in search of double-brined pickles and imported tangerines that Katherine was painfully craving. He enjoyed caring for her and making her feel happy. They were on occasion seen giggling and smiling to each other as if they had a language that only they shared. Spring soon arrived and with it came the final days of Katherine's pregnancy. Ashton cared for her as if it were his own child that she was carrying. He absolutely prohibited her to do anything even remotely strenuous so she just sat in her cushioned chair and call upon Ashton when she needed anything.

"Ashton, I would like to go for a walk in the gardens. Could you fetch me something to put over my shoulders? It looks a bit chilly out there." She gave a longing look to the budding topiaries through the French-style doors. Ashton gave her a disapproving stare but silently complied. They were soon walking in the fresh sunlit rose garden arm in arm. The morning sun was warm and there were no signs left of the heavy winter remaining other than an occasional patch of waterlogged soil left over from the melting ice. Ashton knew, as he had so many times before, that Katherine was contemplating something of extreme importance. Katherine stopped near a blossoming tea rose and turned to Ashton. "I am not going to marry Matthew."

Though this unexpected statement took him aback, he could see the seriousness in her eyes. "Why?" Ashton stated, as if he didn't already know the answer. Although this is secretly what he wanted, he knew that she must marry Matthew for her benefit. He had always known this and he damned his very existence for allowing himself to become so attached to her.

"I know that you don't want me as your wife, but I cannot possibly marry a man if I am completely in love with another," she stated matter-of-factly.

For months Ashton and Katherine's affections had intensified to where they seemed inseparable. He wholeheartedly tried to keep a distance, but his devotion for her had made it nearly impossible. He couldn't help but to be present in her life during the most difficult position she had ever been in.

Ashton carefully chose his words knowing the fragile state that his dear mistress was in currently. "Katherine, you must marry Matthew. I am not right for you. I wish I could make you understand." It pained Ashton to speak these words again. He had spoken them once before unconvincingly, how was he supposed to speak them now and have her believe them?

"Ashton, why do you continue to deny me your love? Your words mean nothing to me. You can't possibly say these things and mean it!" She was so furious that her hands were beginning to shake. "Is this because you are still in love with that other woman?" He suddenly felt very uncomfortable.

"How did you know about her?" He was uneasy with this sort of conversation.

"On Christmas, you were very drunk and told me everything. Is she the real reason that you won't marry me?" She had that familiar pouty look on her face.

"Katherine, that relationship ended a long time ago. She's married with many children now. But I learned a valuable lesson from her. The rich marry the rich and the poor marry everyone else. This is the way that it has always been. It is not my place to challenge that."

"How dare you not want to be with me at all costs? I don't care about being rich or poor and I don't want to marry Matthew because I am in love with you. Nothing that you say can change that!" She seemed to be increasingly short of breath.

"Katherine, please calm down. I just want you to have what is best for you. A man of Matthew's position can care for you; give you anything that you need. I cannot. I've told you that before. I'm sorry, but I just cannot. If I could change the way things are, I most definitely would. I would be rich, younger, and more handsome. I would offer you all of the luxuries that you need. But I simply cannot. Please understand me." Ashton's voice was grave and merely a hoarse whisper at this point. "You will find happiness with him and I will force myself to find it without you."

Katherine could no longer contain her anger. She pounded both fists into Ashton's chest. "How could you say that? I love you and you are just going to throw me away. You selfish bastard!"

Ashton had never seen Katherine so infuriated. "Katherine, please, you must calm down."

Before he had finished his sentence, he saw an alarming look in Katherine's face and she fell to her knees. She immediately lurched forward holding her belly.

"Katie, are you all right?" His heart pounded as he took her into his arms.

"Ashton, something is happening, there is so much pain!" She then let out another groan, much louder this time. The housemaids had heard the argument from the kitchens and ran out to investigate. When Katherine screamed for the third time, they followed Ashton's instructions and headed back to prepare. Ashton knew that it was time to retreat back to the house, the baby was about to arrive.

With the help of some nearby gardeners, Ashton carried Katherine back to the manor. The house staff that had seen them come in from the garden alerted Mr. and Mrs. Kenningston. "The baby is coming! Boil some water and fetch some whiskey." The house was once again brimming with excitement. Soon it seemed that the whole house was in Katherine's room.

Ashton calmly began directing commands at the onlookers. "Please, we must clear this room. Ann, draw some more hot water and gather some towels. Mrs. Kenningston, help me get her into her nightgown, it will be more comfortable for her." Mrs. Kenningston quickly headed for the dresser and retrieved a gown. "No, not that one, she prefers the rose colored one."

Katherine again began to moan loudly. "Ashton, I can't stand the pain. Help me!"

Ashton patted her forehead with a cool cloth and resumed disrobing her. "This will all be over before you know it, dear." Mrs. Kenningston looked as if she were very lightheaded. Katherine screamed aloud this time. He kissed the top of her head and arranged the pillows behind her. "Remember what I told you; just try to concentrate breathing deeply. It is important that you try not to get too excited." Katherine began breathing as he said and appeared instantly calmer.

While Katherine was resting, Ann took the time to ask

Ashton how he knew so much about childbirth. She was taken with his calmness and knowledge on what was a purely feminine task. He told her how he and his father had helped one of the servant girls from many years ago have her child since she could not afford a physician. Word had gotten out about him being a natural at the subject and he began to assist his father, until he died, helping some of the local poor families with various health needs. His father began to purchase medical books with his meager wages and was soon doing everything from mending bones to suturing up minor wounds.

In fact, Ashton's first encounter with Katherine was when his father asked him to accompany him to the manor to suture a wound on her foot from broken glass. She was but a child then, though she tolerated the procedure magnificently. Ashton was amazed with her strength and courage. It was soon thereafter that Ashton's father was taken by influenza and Ashton took his father's place at the manor. Nearly half the household was afflicted with the illness and Ashton proved his worth and talents caring for the family and staff.

"Ashton!" Katherine screamed, grimacing with pain. It was time to push.

Ashton positioned her legs and then instructed her to begin pushing. "Push, Katherine, I can see the baby's head." She began to bear down.

In what seemed like an eternity, though barely a few minutes, Ashton held up a beautiful baby girl. Katherine cried with joy as she held her child. Ashton beamed as if she were his own. The baby immediately opened her crystal blue eyes and stared at him quietly. Suddenly, there was a mystified look on Katherine's face. "Katherine, what's wrong?"

She looked at Ashton. "Oh nothing, it's just the blueness of the baby's eyes, I've seen that glorious color before. I just can't remember where. It seems unusual for such a small child to have eyes that color and look at this small mark on her cheek. I hope it fades right away."

Ashton bent down and lovingly kissed Katherine, and then kissed the baby's tiny forehead. "She's positively beautiful, just like her mother. What are you going to name her?" Ashton asked.

Katherine softly replied, "I would like to name her Julianne, after your father, Julian. With your permission, of course."

Ashton quickly turned and faced the window so that Katherine would not see the tears forming in his eyes. "Yes, I would be honored."

Mrs. Kenningston stared at her daughter holding the newborn and knew that it was time to put their plan into action. She was not going to let her only daughter be the center of gossip and rumors so early in her life.

That night as Ashton prepared a light dinner to take up to Katherine, Mr. Kenningston approached Ashton in the kitchen. "Ashton, I've considered you my friend for many years. You have been loyal in every way and therefore it makes it hard for me to tell you what I need to say."

Ashton could see that the kind Mr. Kenningston had been crying.

"It is pertinent that Katherine marries Matthew, politically and socially. I know that Katie will not marry him because she is in love with you. This is just so complicated; I only hope that you understand how difficult this is for me. I am releasing you from my employ and I am prepared to pay you handsomely."

Ashton stared at Mr. Kenningston in disbelief. "I couldn't possibly leave Katherine and the baby. She is very vulnerable right now and it could be detrimental to her health to put her through so much grief. I am aware that she is in love with me; I am not ashamed to admit that her love is reciprocated. I realize that she must marry Matthew but I couldn't possibly leave her yet."

Mr. Kenningston began to show anger in his face. "Ashton, I'm not asking you to leave, I'm telling you to leave." His voice lowered in secrecy. "There is another matter that we must first discuss. I want you to take the baby with you."

Ashton glared at Mr. Kenningston, stunned. "You've gone mad."

Mr. Kenningston continued to speak. "We cannot allow Katie to enter a marriage toting an illegitimate child in her arms."

Ashton threw the metal serving tray onto the counter, the porcelain serving set shattering loudly. "You told her we would say it was a cousin who had been orphaned. You can't possibly change that now!"

Mr. Kenningston shook his head. "I know that is what I had said, but what if word got out? Matthew surely wouldn't marry her then. Nor would anybody else. Maisy and I have discussed this matter and we both decided that you would be the best person to care for the child. Maybe someday, when Katherine has a family of her own, you may return. We could tell her that you married and the child's mother passed. We could tell her anything that you want. We just want Katherine to be happy. She is too young to handle a new marriage and deal with a newborn. Matthew would surely be suspicious of their bond. Ashton, you must understand."

Ashton knew that Katherine wouldn't marry Matthew because of the love they shared. He contemplated the offer and started to think of what would be best for her. She had suffered so much heartbreak already; she needed to be able to put this all behind her now. His conscious was heavy. "If I accept your offer, how will you explain our disappearance to Katherine?" Ashton was already beginning to regret his contemplation of the absurd arrangement.

"It will be devastating to her as well as ourselves, but we will tell her that little Julianne perished in her sleep." Mr. Kenningston looked tired.

Ashton winced. "And what about me, how will you explain my disappearance?" Ashton was already missing her. He wanted to run to her and hold her for one last moment, but knew that he would not be able to refrain from telling her everything.

"We will tell her that you did not want to stand in her way of marrying Matthew. We will tell her that you were so overtaken with grief from the loss of the baby that you left on your own recognizance. Left the manor forever because of your misery in search of a new life, a happy life. Katherine is resilient; we both know that. She will heal quickly." Mr. Kenningston began to weep for what he was about to put his daughter through. "Go, man, leave at once. Ann has begun to pack your things and I have sent word to London. They will have an apartment and necessities for the baby waiting for you. We will send word to you periodically on Katherine's progress, it's the least that we can do."

Ashton left the room quickly and gathered the rest of his things. Ann brought Julianne to him, already bundled and in a basket. There was a small bottle of goat's milk and changing towels in the carrier. They left the manor unnoticeably just as the sun was setting. Ashton turned as the coach drove away, hoping to glimpse one last time the only woman he would ever truly love.

Chapter Twelve

KATHERINE AWOKE EARLY THE next morning, just before dawn. She was still fatigued from giving birth, but wanted to see her precious Julianne. "Ashton? I want to see the baby, could you bring her to me please?" Her voice was weak still, so she called out again. "Ashton? Bring me Julianne; she's probably hungry by now." Katherine was surprised when it was her mother who had entered her room, her eyes reddened and puffy. Katherine knew right away that her mother had been crying. "Mum? What's upsetting you? Surely the baby is all right? Where's Ashton?"

Her mother did not answer her as the fear began to rise in Katherine; she knew at once that something was deadly wrong. Mrs. Kenningston could do nothing but shake her head in sorrow. Though she knew that the baby wasn't dead, she was still mourning for the loss of possibly never seeing her grandchild again.

Katherine sat upright, staring deeply at her mother. She

found herself whispering as she spoke. "Please, tell me it isn't so, tell me there isn't anything wrong with my Julianne...please." She knew at once that the baby was gone. Mrs. Kenningston held her grief-stricken daughter as she cried aloud.

When she had begun to calm, Mrs. Kenningston then told he that Ashton also was gone. More than her young mind could handle, Katherine then just rolled over and stared at the early morning sky. She could not even speak. She would remain speechless for the next few days, unable to leave the securities of her own room. She vowed to herself that she would never remove the small locket containing her daughter's hair from her neck. The locket that was given to her by Ashton was now a tribute to the only two things that she ever loved, and only death would truly separate the two.

The postman brought word that Matthew would arrive one week from today. Katherine spoke for the first time since the death of her child and the loss of her dearest companion, Ashton. "What color shall the flowers be?"

Janice stunned that Katherine spoke, soon had Mrs. Kenningston at her bedside. "Katherine, dear, did you speak to Janice?"

Katherine turned her head to her mother and with the dazed look remaining in her eyes, repeated slowly, "I asked what color should the flowers be?"

Janice glanced at Mr. Kenningston hoping that she understood what Katherine meant. "I don't understand, what flowers?" Mrs. Kenningston was beginning to think that her daughter was showing signs of mental illness.

"Ashton and Julianne are both gone, all I have left is Matthew. I want to know what color of flowers I shall have for the wedding." Janice and Mrs. Kenningston in unison ran to Katherine's bedside and held her in their arms. They were overjoyed that Katherine was feeling better. They both knew that Matthew was just what she needed to put her awful past behind her.

The house was once again in the midst of excitement. Maids and servants scurrying through the halls readying every detail that they could think of for the big day. Though Katherine had not fully recovered quite yet, she seemed to enjoy preparing the wedding plans, or so she appeared. Katherine had always dealt with tragedy by simply pretending that the events never happened. On the outside, she seemed to have returned to her old self, her beautiful waistline had returned, and she had that fanciful twinkle in her eye once again. She looked as though she was the girl she once was, except for the absence of her once constant smile. Katherine, who at one time seemed to laugh on a whim, now seemed to rarely outwardly show any true emotion at all.

The tailors were at the house for most of the week, preparing her gown and accessories. The caterers had been notified and were seen at the house with last minute requisitions. Katherine worked with the planners that her father had sent for from London, finishing the last details of the wedding. Matthew would be arriving tomorrow evening for the engagement dinner. All of Katherine's friends from town, some of her relatives from London, and Matthew's parents were all going to be present for the feast.

The next evening came and only Mrs. Kenningston noticed that Katherine did not completely seem herself. She dressed in a formal gown for dinner and headed for dinner. All of the guests had arrived and were seated in the grand dining room awaiting their guest of honor. As she descended the staircase and entered the room, all eyes were on her. She could barely stand to face any of them for fear that they may discover her secret. Katherine was especially concerned that Matthew would somehow read her thoughts and learn of her hidden loss. She made certain not to make eye contact with anyone if possible. After quickly seating herself next to Matthew, she heard her father clear his throat loudly as if to gain everyone's attention. Mr. Kenningston rose and ceremoniously toasted to the couple, reminding himself to appear as normal as possible. Katherine fidgeted with her hands as she always did when she was nervous, thanking him for gesture. The entire party cheered the couple and began their meal. Matthew at once noticed the change in Katherine. She seemed different, distant. She suffered the entire dinner without so much as saying a single word to him. Expressing not even the usual pleasantries that he had formally been used to. Mrs. Kenningston noticed Matthew's concern and made a polite comment to the guests about how Katherine was recovering from a nasty bout of the flu. She assured them that Katherine would be healthy in no time and would be perfectly fit for the wedding.

Afterward, the party retired to the patio for drinks and music. The familiar scent of lilies filled her senses. The warm breeze arising from the meadow beyond comforted Katherine and strangely she found herself smiling. She was instantly taken back to one year ago. The memories of her and Ashton planning shopping, gardening, entertaining, flooded her mind. If only she could return to that fateful day that she rode alone by the stream side and change what would be her destiny. Things would be different. Now there was no Ashton to watch over her and there would be no rescuing her from what she feared most tonight.

Matthew, unnerved by Katherine's stoic behavior, asked her to dance immediately. He wanted every guest in the party to lay eyes on his beautiful bride-to-be. He secretly thought lustily about what he was going to do to her in a few short days. Her bosom seemed even more full than he had remembered, calling out to him from beneath her dress. The softness of her hair, the fresh scent of her skin, all would be his for the taking before the end of the week.

113

Katherine found herself compelled to stare intently at something in the west pasture as she tried to ignore the unwanted attentions of her husband-to-be, Matthew. She knew that the stable boys were excused hours ago yet it appeared that someone was standing in the tall grass...watching her. The blades rolling like waves, making the figure appear to be standing knee deep in a golden sea. The sun was setting low in glorious pinks and reds behind the figure so that only a wavering outline of the person could be seen. Katherine decided that it must be her imagination, who would possibly be standing in the fields amongst the horses at this hour?

She immediately was startled by the stern voice that came from behind her. "Katherine, my dear, you seem so quiet. Did I say something to offend you this evening?" It was Matthew and he was staring at her questioningly. His bold tailored suit screamed arrogance and secretly disgusted her.

She managed to raise her eyes to meet his and answered reassuringly. "I'm just tired, with all of the events as of late." She managed to fake a smile for his benefit.

He leaned close to her ear so that only she would hear. "You had better rest up, my dear, I have a few things myself in store for you." He pressed his body closer to hers so that she would feel his rock hard manhood against her waist.

She was instantly mortified. Nor could she believe that she had agreed to marry such a monster. Suddenly, she felt like her life was just one tragedy after another and could see no way to end this tragic cycle. Wondering at this point if life was worth living at all, she once again stared into the distance, hoping to glimpse the mirage that was before hiding somewhere in the sunset. Katherine saw just what she expected—nothing at all.

"Come now, dear, rest your feet. You look as though you've seen a ghost." Mrs. Kenningston saw her daughter's distracted expression and insisted that she rest.

"Yes, dear Katherine, you rest awhile. I think that maybe we shall take a walk in the gardens later." He gracefully bowed as he kissed her hand, giving her an unseen wink. She felt unexpectedly repulsed by this action. Seating herself hopelessly in a chair next to her mother, she loudly gulped her champagne from the fine crystal glass and immediately asked for another. She thought that a few drinks might help her somehow tolerate this dreadful night.

Her now married childhood friend, Teresa, noticed too that something was amiss about Katherine. She watched the interaction between Matthew and Katherine from a distance for a moment and then discreetly approached Katherine with her concerns. "Katherine, may I speak to you for a moment, privately?"

Katherine, thankful to escape Matthew's watchful eye, followed Teresa to the pool area.

Teresa found a spot far enough from the others that their conversation wouldn't be accidentally overheard. "I may be speaking out of turn here, but I sense something isn't quite right between you and Matthew."

Katherine contemplated telling Teresa everything, but refrained from doing so at the moment, fearing that her friend would only think less of her because of her carelessness. "I'm just nervous, I suppose. I'm sure that you experience these same emotions when you were preparing for your own wedding."

Teresa stared at Katherine unconvinced.

Katherine acknowledged the disbelieving look in her friend's eyes and decided to selectively tell her at least a portion of the reasons behind her sorrow. Gently leaning toward her friend, she spoke in nearly a whisper, afraid that she would somehow be heard and her secret discovered. "Teresa, you mustn't repeat to anyone what I am about to tell you."

Teresa nodded, eager to find the source of Katherine's distress.

"A year ago, I fell in love with Ashton." It was unclear at that time if what Katherine was saying was true.

Teresa gasped. "Ashton? The butler?" She thought for certain that Katherine was mocking her. "Come now, Katherine, I'm serious. You really haven't been yourself."

Katherine spoke, quieter this time. She leaned toward her friend; voice nearly just a whisper against her ear. "I swear to you, Teresa, that what I tell you is not in jest. I loved Ashton, and I know that at some point, he loved me."

Teresa, though now somewhat confused and surprised, felt genuine sympathy for her dear friend. "Oh, Katherine, I am so sorry. He is gone now; you must concentrate solely on Matthew!" She embraced Katherine. "I know that you are a strong person and you must find a way to move on."

As they turned down the path to the manor, Katherine realized how much Teresa's statement was true.

It was in the late evening when all of the guests were chatting among each other, that Matthew asked Katherine to take a walk with him. Katherine stared at the cobblestones beneath her fine leather shoes, praying to God that she find a reason to be excused from Matthew's presence.

"Please excuse me, but I would like to borrow this lovely lady for a few moments to enjoy some of this glorious moonlight. It was, after all, the moonlight that introduced us." The crowd of women nearby swooned though Katherine's own heart sank. She did not want to spend a moment alone with him. He too seemed…different.

Nevertheless, she soon found herself strolling arm in arm with Matthew down the garden path. "Katherine, my dear, you have been acting positively strange this evening. Please tell me what is going on, I insist." He reached up and softly touched her lips.

She thought quickly of a lie to cover up for her strange behavior, forcing a laugh to seemingly dismiss his insinuation. "Seriously, Matthew, you are mistaken. I just have been busy with the wedding plans; these things can be quite worrisome at times. Besides, Mother told you that I have been ill." She found herself once again wearing an unmistakably false smile. There would be no Ashton to save her this time.

"I don't believe a word you are saying. Do you really think that I am so dim? You are still upset about your beloved Ashton's sudden departure." He suddenly had a violent grip on her arm.

She was alarmed by this action and stared widely at him. "Matthew, what are you talking about? Please, you must stop this instant. You are hurting my arm." She twisted her wrist, trying to free herself from his stern grip. "How dare you say such things." She broke free from his grasp and began to rapidly head back to the party, hoping that he would not follow her.

"Katherine, stop." He caught up with her and turned her around by the waist, kissing her roughly on the lips. Katherine allowed herself to kiss him back out of respect for her husband-to-be, but couldn't help feel that she was betraying the memory of Ashton. They were both soon heading back to the manor where some of the guests were beginning to leave though no one noticed that Katherine was quite shaken.

"Well, my dear lady, I too should be off. I have some dealings of my own to take care of before our big day." Kissing her on the cheek, he whispered gently into her ear, "I'm sorry, dear lady, I shall not let it happen again." He then bid the rest of the party good evening and left for his coach. Katherine was relieved to see him leave down the long roadway to town. She politely waited for the last guest to leave and then retired quietly to her room.

Katherine refused to let any of the housemaids take Ashton's place. She now took care of all of her own baths, dressing, and hair. It was as if she were shutting everyone that she held dear out of her life. Alone in her quarters, she slowly got undressed and peered out the window to the pasture. She

117

could see that the stable boys had forgotten to put her horse in the stall and it was grazing merrily in the west pasture beneath the fading moonlight. She wondered if Matthew would let her keep Tom at their new house.

After a few moments of contemplation, she found her eyes focusing on a vague shadow directly below her window. She felt as if she were seeing visions everywhere lately. Still quickly she blew out her lamp so that she could get a better view of the darkness and could just begin to make out what seemed to be someone standing at some distance below her window, fearing that this time there may actually be someone watching her. She rubbed her tired eyes in disbelief because the outline of this shadow looked strikingly like—Ashton. Her heart leapt as she tried to focus through the darkness once again on the shadow, but it was gone.

She turned and sat on her bed for a moment wondering out loud, finally dismissing the shadow as just another illusion conjured up by her weary heart. She knew that she was still in a fragile state and that the mind could sometimes play tricks to ease the pain. She placed her head on her pillow and dreamed of Ashton and the few precious moments she had with her beautiful child, secretly wishing that Ashton would indeed return to her side, removing her from all of the pains that she foresaw in her near future.

Chapter Thirteen

KATHERINE WAS AWOKEN BY the familiar sounds of the summer birds chirping in the nearby birch trees. Today was her wedding day. It would be the day that she will start a new life as Mrs. Matthew Wordly, a life destined to be without Ashton. The maids, at much protest from Katherine, insisted that they help bathe her and ready her for the big day. Her dress was finished just in time for the big event. She chose a simple yet elegant gown, all the while feeling somewhat guilty that it was such an innocently pure white. She touched the locket that still hung from her neck, hoping that it would give her even the slightest feeling of comfort. She had spent all her life waiting for this day, now she wanted nothing more than for it to be over.

Mrs. Kenningston had been at the church for most of the day helping the decorators with the last minute preparations. Practically everyone in town was going to be present for their union. Mr. Kenningston, already fully dressed in his formal attire, was at the breakfast table ignoring his eggs while intently reading the morning newspaper. Katherine tiptoed into the room and helping herself to a pastry and tea when she heard her father comment angrily on the headlining story. "I can't believe it; another young girl was beaten last night in town. What is this world coming to? These people want to revolt against the tax, but don't have the intellect to go through the proper channels to change things. What do they expect to accomplish by savagely beating little girls?" His face was completely red and his fists were balled so tight that they appeared to have gone pale.

"Father, have you heard anything from Ashton yet?" Katherine interrupted, trying to quickly change the subject.

Mr. Kenningston appeared taken aback and was speechless for a moment, obviously not aware that Katherine had entered the room. "Well, darling, uh, no. I haven't heard from him. He hasn't sent post to us for quite some time now. These things just happen, dear. He only did it for your own good and you must respect him for that. The man had dreams of his own, surely you understand." Mr. Kenningston tried to appear engrossed in his newspaper. Katherine remained silent. She wanted more than anything to tell her father that she would never love anyone else, but knew that it would be of no use. Her father wanted her to marry Matthew and there would be no way of getting around it.

The quaint English cathedral was filled with all the local townsfolk. Katherine had been placed in her gown and had once again managed to take the breath away from anyone in her company. 'Magnificent' was the only word that her father could manage to mumble. The maids fussed about her with a few final preparations in her dressing room, though Katherine took no notice in them, clearly deep thought. Her father knew deep within his own heart that she was thinking of Ashton, and no one else. He was beginning to feel guilty for putting her through this after all she had endured and imagined how things would be different if he were in her place. It was then that he realized he had made a mistake in all the choices that he had made for her thus far, but it was far too late to change them. "Dear girl, I know that we pressured you into this. With time, you will see that it is for the best. Your mother felt the same way on our wedding day and just look how things turned out." He winked reassuringly at his daughter.

The music began to play as Katherine remembered what her dearest friend had once told her: "Whenever you feel like the world is handing you too much, just remember to smile and nod like you mean it. Don't ever let them see your fear." She was only ten years old when Ashton told her this and she thought it strange that the memory had surfaced now. Peeking through the dressing room doorway, she heard the soft melody of the wedding march begin. The orchestra had started and this was to mark the beginning of all things anew. She felt as if there was a great stone at the pit of her stomach when she gracefully approached the aisles full of guests. It took all of her courage and strength to resist the overwhelming urge to run directly out of the church when she spotted Matthew down the aisle, standing stoically between the waxed oak pews. She smiled blankly at the wedding guests; she was not about to let them see her pain on what was supposed to be her happiest day of young womanhood. She had to marry Matthew so that she could manage some kind of life from her shambled past.

The wedding was the same as any other, though of coarse, twice as extravagant. Katherine mumbled through the ceremony, stumbling on the lines that she had memorized, all the while telling herself that it was all just a bad dream. Her voice quivered as she spoke those final words 'I do,' feeling dishonest not only to her guests, but also to herself. She was fated to profess her love this very day to a man she hardly knew. Her entire life had become inundated with deceit.

They dined with the wedding party and guests and

reluctantly danced most of the night. Though Katherine's thoughts were never far from Ashton or Julianne, this was her new life and she knew that she must make the best of the situation. She concentrated on smiling pretty to the guests and her new husband, not forgetting her 'pleases' and 'thank yous.'

Afterwards, she rode to her new house, built especially for Matthew and his bride-to-be. Her things had not yet arrived from the manor, nor did she care. The new house staff was all waiting at the drive when the coaches arrived. They bowed in unison to their lady of the house in respect. So many unfamiliar faces, so many unfamiliar things, still Katherine held her head up high, once again in Ashton and Julianne's memory. That was the one thing that Matthew's world could not take from her.

As they entered the room, Matthew's demeanor changed from jovial to menacing. "What is the matter, girl? You haven't said one word to me all day. You're not exactly the young git I remember." Katherine felt shocked that he would be so cold to her on their first night as man and wife. Noticing that she was hurt by his words he smiled and spoke harshly to her as if she were one of his horses. "Well nonetheless, I didn't marry you for the chitchat." He eyed her slender body once again openly and grinned.

She felt shameful and glared at him for making her feel that way. "I'm just tired. I told you that this wedding has had me busy the last few weeks." She once again attempted to appear upbeat and chipper, something that she had rehearsed for this very moment, looking around at the magnificent furnishings of her new house. "Well, the house is lovely. I'm sure I will feel quite at home here." She began to walk around the parlor and admire the bright paintings that were carefully hung on all four walls.

"There is a pool out beyond the garden, in case you feel like taking any…midnight swims." He ran his finger softly down the length of her bare shoulder, creating shivers of disgust up her spine. She was very uncomfortable with the intimacy of his statement. How did he know that she had a love of swimming? She knew that she would never indulge him in something so private in any of her correspondences while he was away. Perplexed, she tried to conceal her unease by asking for a lengthy tour of the house. He had written her many times explaining the many adjustments and additions to the house that he had made awaiting her arrival but she just couldn't recall telling him that she enjoyed swimming after dusk. The house was built and given to them by his father as a wedding gift for the new couple.

"This is the kitchen. We have six service staff to attend to us. Penne at the lead. I'm sure that you will find her services quite admirable, as do I. I have instructed that they serve us our morning meal in our sleeping quarters for the next few days." He then whispered crudely in her ear, "It will give us a few extra moments in the mornings to really get to know each other." Katherine dreaded the evening to come. She was still recovering from the birth of Julianne and didn't know if her body was capable of performing the marital duties in question. They continued to tour the beautiful house and Katherine tried to appear deeply interested in the various lamps, tables, and vases so that she could have a reason to step away from Matthew when she felt him eyeing her. She immediately decided that the house would be suitable for her liking though the company within it would not.

When they reached the large window in the east wing of the house, Katherine was delighted to see three large, freshly painted stables directly outside. "I will show you the stables later. I will, of course, send for your horse, Tom, in a few days."

Once again she was taken aback by what he had said and now felt compelled to question him. "How did you know that I had a horse named Tom, or that I enjoy riding for that matter?" She was having a difficult time controlling her anger.

"Well," Matthew seemed to stumble, "I spoke with your dear Ashton by post while I was away and gathered some pertinent information that I thought would help us become more acquainted after the wedding. I wanted you to be comfortable right away in your new home." His smile disarmed her somewhat but she still had the feeling that something was amiss. Ashton would undoubtedly have said something to her before his unexpected departure if he was receiving post from the likes of Matthew.

"Oh, I see." She felt a rush of embarrassment come over her, though she still felt that something wasn't quite right. "Thank you for your consideration. Yes, I would like Tom to be here. I enjoy riding very much, though I haven't had the time as of late." Katherine managed to smile convincingly back at Matthew.

While resting once again in the parlor, Matthew poured her some champagne. "Have some of this, you seem to be a tad uptight. I understand how uncomfortable you must feel. This is quite different from the manor and you aren't used to being so far away from your parents." This sudden turn of compassion confused Katherine. "You will be happy here, I will assure that." He poured himself another glass and seated himself next to her. "Are you ready to retire for the night?"

Katherine realized why Matthew's demeanor had softened and her heart bounded in her chest. She new that it was time to dishonor her loyalty to Ashton just as he had done to her by leaving. It was time to be a wife to Matthew. He led her to the bedroom and before the hour was up, the marriage was painfully consummated.

Chapter Fourteen

THE REMAINING WEEKS OF the spring came and went in a flash and the waning days of summer were once again soon upon them. Unnoticeably, another fall had gradually arrived and most of Katherine's days were spent arranging the house with her various belongings. She felt as though she was beginning to feel somewhat comfortable in the house, despite Matthew's disturbing presence. The house staff seemed to be much more distant than the staff at her parents' house, but tended to their duties magnificently. Although very attentive to her needs, they just didn't have that warm friendly way about them as Ann, Janice and, of course, Ashton had.

Katherine was soon adorning her own garden with the roses that she loved so much, she had ample time to read and study about the care for then while Matthew was gone for hours, sometimes days at work. Pruning and tending to the roses was a mindless chore that kept her occupied within the lonely confines of the house grounds. Matthew gave her whatever she wanted to keep the long days while he was away working, contently occupied. She was often seen riding her horse in her own pasture, and had resumed her music lessons from before. On occasion, she would have visitors over from church for an afternoon tea, but unfortunately Matthew began to question her immensely about who was there, what they had talked about, and any other paranoid thing that he could think of. It wasn't long before Matthew's insecurities had completely secluded Katherine from her friends and family without anyone from the outside realizing it. She had also taken in a love of sewing and embroidery, something that she had despised until now. She found a strange sense of comfort in the repetitive task. Ashton had tried to show her many times before how to do this delicate handiwork, but she had always found it boring and dull. She soon became keenly interested in the craft and had actually become quite good at it.

It was an extremely warm late fall morning when Katherine had used up her last spool of Yevette Mauve thread. She normally would wait until Matthew or one of the house servants traveled to town to pick up more of this distinct yarn, but she was feeling particularly bored and needing a change of scenery. "Penne! I am going to have one of the stable boys take me into town to gather supplies for my stitch work!" Katherine called out knowing that the maid would more than likely be close by watching her as her master had undoubtedly instructed.

Penne, the staunch elderly maid, was soon by her side and was wiping her wet hands hastily on her apron. "No, madam, I'm sorry but I simply cannot allow this. It simply is not permissible," she stated, acting as though she was out of breath. After all, she had to appear as if she was busily engaged in her cleaning duties.

Katherine stopped in the middle of the foyer, unsure of her interpretation of Penne's statement. "Excuse me, my ears are playing tricks again. What did you say?" Katherine was certain that she had misunderstood the elderly maid's comment.

"Mr. Wordly has instructed us to, under no circumstances, allow you to travel the township without his presence. We must respect his wishes." Penne stood steadfast at the doorway, determined to follow her master's request.

Fire instantly burned in Katherine's heart. A sudden courage flooded into Katherine and she took a few steps toward the servant. Remaining in composure, she stated calmly, but firmly, "It seems that you have forgotten that I am the lady of this house, and I will now allow my servants to be insubordinate in any way while I am living under this roof. So if you will please step aside, madam, I will return sometime around midday." Katherine lifted her skirts defiantly and headed to the stables.

She furiously entered the dark stables and called out for John, the stable boy who often drove the new couple to town. "John? I need to go into town today, will you ready the coach?"

Strangely, she did not find the young stable hand attending his hay pile as he had always seemed to be working at when she was ready to go for a ride. While awaiting an answer, she distantly overheard two men talking in low voices around the corner of the hay storage wall. She bravely followed the voices; still furious with the way her current servants had begun to treat her, trying to quickly locate John. She had some difficulty seeing, though she was squinting her eyes to see through the dusty, dark walkway. As she turned the corner, she saw a large man talking to John who looked alarmingly familiar. "John, who is this? Is he a new hire?"

Katherine stopped immediately at the entrance because she at once remembered where she had known this man before. She gasped at the realization that it was Timothy Barnes, one of her attackers on that dark summer night over a year ago. Horrified, Katherine let out a scream and took a few steps backward,

SARA DE ARMON

tripping over a hayfork leaning against a post and instantly falling backwards to the plank board floor.

Swiftly, the familiar man turned and fled out the side door of the stables. John nervously helped Katherine to her feet and tried to calm her. "Mrs. Wordly, what is the matter, you look positively terrified!"

Katherine turned to him. "That was Timothy Barnes; he had...stolen my coin purse last summer. I... I'm sure it was him." Her head was spinning with panic.

John was unusually silent for a moment and then stated, "No, madam, you must be mistaken, that was Peter Stone. He is Mr. Wordly's handyman. He fixes things around the house and runs errands occasionally. I'm sorry that he gave you such a fright, but I assure you that he is most definitely a harmless sort."

Katherine began to feel a little more at ease but addressed the stable boy with some skepticism. "If that were so, how is it that I hadn't seen him on the estate before?"

John once again appeared to be thinking of what to say next. "He just isn't much into socializing, that's all. Likes to keep to himself."

She began to come to the realization that maybe she had indeed made a mistake. The heavy air and shadows of the stables could have easily altered her vision, making Mr. Stone appear to be someone he was not. She began to feel silly. "I'm sorry, John, I don't know what I was thinking. I obviously need to get away from this place for a few hours, which is why I came out here in the first place." She vigorously brushed the hay from her long skirts. Breathless, she stated her request. "Would you mind taking me to town to shop for a while?"

Before she had even finished speaking, John had hastily guided her out of the stables. She noticed that he kept glancing strangely over his shoulder as if he had forgotten something, but thought that she was just imaging things again. Her mind had been increasingly more fragile with each passing month, and she felt as if her sanity was slowly slipping away from her with each passing moment.

It had been many months since there had been any problems with the locals so Katherine was not afraid to go into town without her husband in the daytime. Although John was a young man close to her own young age, she was certain that he was capable of protecting her if need be, considering his large build. She still felt angry for Penne trying to keep her at the house, and thought about inquiring to Matthew that they replace her as soon as the opportunity arose. She absolutely refused to allow her servants to make her feel like a prisoner in her own house.

Once she arrived in town, she gave John some money and instructed him to pick up some miscellaneous items for the house. He was to meet her in the park in precisely two hours giving them plenty of time to return home before Matthew returned. She felt peculiarly lighthearted and free as she browsed about the bustling shops. It had been sometime since she had been to town and was enjoying herself immensely. She had seen many of her past friends, including the now hopelessly pregnant Teresa, that were also out enjoying the temperate fall air. Even the Welles were out for brunch at one of the sidewalk cafés that were so popular among the local socialites. She bid them good day and continued on her way through the lively streets of town. Soon she finished her shopping and headed toward the park to wait for John. She walked leisurely, enjoying the glorious autumn foliage that lined the downtown streets this time of year.

When she arrived at the awaiting coach, she was surprised to see Matthew standing at its side. His face was surly and he had an irate look to him when she approached, though he no doubt appeared to be deeply interested in his newspaper. She quickly put on her best false smile in efforts to disarm him before she approached his side.

"Matthew, what in heavens are you doing here?" She acted

as though she did not notice his annoyance.

He at once began speaking to her as though she were a child in need of scolding. He spoke loudly and she could see people peering at them from the neighboring shops at the disorder. "You are absolutely forbidden to come into town without me by your side!" He irritably threw his newspaper to the ground.

Katherine glanced around to see just how many people were staring at them. Unfortunately the streets were quite busy today. "Matthew, I was gathering some supplies for my embroidery. I am hardly an invalid. I most definitely do not need an escort to go shopping." Katherine spoke in a low tone so that the passers-by could not hear every last detail of their conversation.

"I am your husband and you will do as I say. I will not have you coming into town to meet the likes of 'him.'" Katherine was shocked by her husband's unkind words. She couldn't imagine why he would declare such things to her, and in a public place! She felt overcome by his indignity and began to board the coach to prevent any more embarrassment. As she stepped onto the brass step, she felt a hard shove from directly behind. Matthew had pushed her into the coach and she landed face first on the seat, sharply banging her head. The door was slammed shut behind her and she found herself having trouble focusing her eyes.

"Take her back and don't let this happen again." Katherine could distantly hear Matthew speak angrily to John. The pain that she had in her heart was far worse than the pain that throbbed in her head that day. She softly cried for the entire trip home.

As the coach pulled into the driveway, the clouds overhead were beginning to darken and a low rumbling could be heard in the distance. Katherine did not announce her arrival to the servants and ran unnoticeably to her bedroom instead. She carefully washed the blood from the large lump on the side of her head. After arranging her hair to conceal the wound, she had cried herself dry and now had to spend the rest of the day dreading the arrival of her angry husband. He usually came home just around six o'clock and there were but a few short hours to pull herself together. She was preparing to bathe when Penne knocked on her door telling her that Ann, her parents' maid, had come to visit her. She quickly dressed, happy to have a familiar face to look at.

There was a sharp crack of lightning when Katherine arrived at the door causing her to startle. She opened the door and quickly invited Ann in since Penne rudely did not think to do so. Immediately Katherine excused Penne while they visited uninterrupted though she had a suspicion that she was still nearby listening to the intimate details of their conversation. Ann seemed nervous but happy to see Katherine, all the while Katherine was somewhat bewildered by the unexpected visit. "Ann! How have you been? How I've missed you terribly. Mum tells me that you took an occasional position with a family in town?" She gave Ann a warm hug and asked her to sit with her for a while in the parlor.

"Yes, I suppose that is right. Oh, never mind me, miss, I mean, madam. I brought you some raspberry jam that I remember you liked so much. It is Mr. Ashton's recipe that I came upon while washing out the cupboards last week." She handed the willow basket to Katherine.

Katherine found herself deeply touched by Ann's thoughtfulness. She peeked into the basket at the glorious ruby jars. Anything at all from her past was comforting these trying days. She could remember picking raspberries with Ashton as a child and how furious he would get with her for eating nearly the lot of them before they would return home.

Suddenly, her eyes focused on a bit of parchment sticking out from beneath the cloth napkin. As she reached into the basket to retrieve the note, her gaze met Ann's and the maid slowly shook her head in a 'no' motion. Outside, weather had worked itself up into a strong fall thunderstorm. Katherine understood and calmly sat the basket on the table beside her, thanking Ann for the jam. The maid then rose and stated that she had better make the visit short before the weather made it dangerous to travel back to town. Katherine showed her the door as Penne appeared from nowhere to show her out. The rain was pelting down by this time and there were lightning flashes everywhere. A cool wind burst into the doorway as they opened it. Ann shivered loudly.

"Ann, please take my shawl. It is chilly outside this evening and I think it should help." She placed the shawl around the young maid's shoulders and then walked with her onto the entranceway.

"Thank you." Ann looked as if she were going to say something to Katherine but hesitated then gently curtseyed and boarded the coach.

As Ann began to ride away, Katherine noticed someone standing at the end of the drive. Every few seconds the lightning would illuminate the figure and after a moment, she began to make out who it was. Suddenly feeling faint as she recognized the familiar figure of Ashton, she reached for the railing to steady herself. This time, it was not her imagination. She wanted to run to him but knew better than to do that with Penne watching her every move. Katherine strained her eyes all the while attempting to appear to be waving goodbye to her old friend. She relished every second that her eyes were on him. Penne did not see the figure in the distance as her aging eyes were not as accurate as Katherine's; therefore, Katherine was not worried about the discovery. Her heart seemed to be weighed with sorrow as the long-coated figure waved and boarded the coach that carried the maid. Ashton stood still for a moment, seeming also to savor the few seconds that they shared. She squinted, hoping not to be noticed, at the slowing coach. It seemed that the Ashton was carrying something. Perhaps a package, though at this distance she could not tell, making the moment all the more strange.

After a few moments, Katherine then turned and brushed past the sullen Penne and sat in the parlor next to the elegant basket. She asked the servant to bring her some toast and tea so that she could enjoy a taste of the fresh batch of jams. Penne at once reached for the basket trying to get a better look at its contents, clearly full of suspicion. Katherine instantly pulled it closer to herself telling Penne that she wanted to admire it for a bit longer. Meanwhile, while Penne went into the kitchen to ready the refreshments, Katherine carefully slipped the note into her undergarments. The maid returned promptly and Katherine remained sitting, grinning to herself all the while she ate.

When she had finished, Katherine called to Penne. "Would you draw me a bath? I think that I would like to freshen up before Matthew returns." Katherine hurried to her and Matthew's bedroom and slipped the letter beneath her armoire where it would not be discovered. Penne did as she was instructed all the while unsuspecting of Katherine's oddish behaviors. Katherine was smiling to herself, almost giddy while she climbed the stairs to the master quarters. She knew that even if it were bad news from Ashton, any sign of him would be better than the sadness that surrounded her new life.

The hot bath was steaming, waiting for Katherine to get into it. A glass of red wine was quickly readied at her request, as she needed something to calm her from her day's emotions. Ashton had told her once that one glass of wine was often prescribed to calm the nerves. As soon as Penne left the room, Kathcrine locked the door and retrieved the letter. She undressed, took a few sips from her glass and began to read:

My Dearest Katie,
I am sorry to intrude on your new life but I fear for your safety. I have been watching you secretly for the past six months, whenever possible, and feel that you are now in danger. Please understand my intrusion, but I feel that

it is pertinent that I intervene. I cannot tell you my whereabouts but if you need to contact me, notify Ann. I will come to you anytime, day or night, but be informed, that if I do, it will be to take you away from that place...forever. I am going to make this thing as easy as possible for you. I have some leads on the men who have destroyed your life and I am almost ready to take the evidence to the authorities, I only hope that you will respect me when I am done.

    With truest love,
    Ashton

    Though Katherine felt joy in knowing that Ashton was safe, she was once again puzzled by his actions. What did he mean by watching her? Did he know about the terrible scene that Matthew made in the park that day? Her face was hot with embarrassment. She did not want anyone to know of her poor life choice in husbands. Her life had already been riddled with tragedy, any further embarrassment would only add to this. She did not want to be talked about as the poor Mrs. Wordly, the wife of a rich drunkard. Just as Katherine was finished, Matthew had called up to the room and announced that he was home and dinner was being served.

    Katherine hid the note from her dear friend beneath the armoire once again and put herself in one of her finest dresses. She knew that Matthew would be in bad spirits and she would do what she could to please him this evening to avoid any confrontation.

    Katherine descended the stairway and knew immediately that Matthew had been drinking. The sour smell of whiskey was present even before she entered the room. She practiced her now routine false smile a few times and then walked into the dining room where their plates were set to be served and the maids were waiting patiently for Katherine's presence. Matthew at once noticed the fine dress that she was wearing and made a lewd comment about why she was wearing anything at all. She pretended not to notice and proceeded to sit at the table to enjoy her meal. Matthew quickly began to lecture her about her behavior at town that day and she just sat quietly and listened to him attentively. She knew Matthew's temper enough by now not to annoy him anymore than he already was. She just sat silently and finished her meal, all the while smiling to herself. When the dessert and coffee was finished, Katherine went to bed and let her husband finish his dinner alone and angry.

The next few weeks were spent with Katherine wondering exactly what Ashton had meant. She wanted to be a good wife to Matthew and thought that if she just try to not make him angry, she would not have to worry about his erratic behavior. This, however, was not the case. Matthew's possessiveness and control had increased so that Katherine was now afraid to do anything at all but stay within the grounds of the house and the gardens.

No news from Ashton was taking its toll on Katherine. She decided that the letter was a cruel trick that someone was playing and that it wasn't Ashton who had written the note at all. She was afraid to question her parents about the matter for fear the existence of the note would somehow be discovered by Matthew. The days droned on and she dreamed of the lazy days that she and Ashton used to spend at the Kenningston manor. She didn't realize that she had once had everything that she ever really wanted until it had all gone away.

One day while Katherine was out tending to her blooming garden, she felt as though someone was watching her. Her personal maid had excused herself for a few moments to hang some laundry that she had washed earlier. Katherine had assured her that she would be quite all right without someone watching her and that all she would be doing was removing the spent blooms from her rosebushes.

She heard a soft clank approaching from the direction of the stables and turned to investigate the unfamiliar sound. Her heart sank when she recognized her husband's handyman Peter Stone. Although she was somewhat convinced by the stable boy she had spoken to weeks earlier that this was not one of her attackers, she still had some doubts. It had been over a year since she was attacked and her memory was foggy, but she couldn't help but be shaken by the uncanny resemblance of Peter Stone with Timothy Barnes.

Within moments, Peter was standing directly in front of her and she was beginning to feel the terror rise up within her. "Can I help you with something?" It took all of her strength and courage to try to appear calm. There were already rumors about the house questioning her mental state, and she didn't want to add to this.

"I don't quite know how to tell you this. I have discovered from the others that you are a wonderful and beautiful person. This is why I come to you now. Matthew is a very sick, though very influential man. He is...not exactly who you believe him to be." She was certain that this man was at least a relative of Timothy; she had trouble focusing attentions on what he was saying since she was trying to dismiss the resemblance.

"I'm sorry, I don't know what you mean." Completely perplexed by this time, she began to back slowly away from the man.

"Mr. Wordly isn't the person that you think that he is. You are in danger and I risk my life telling you this. You need to pack your belongings and leave this place. Before he...before you are hurt." Peter looked as though he was about to run at any sound that he heard. He fidgeted with the shovel that he held which only increased Katherine's uneasiness.

"I don't know what you are talking about, but I think that you need to leave before I call for my maid. You clearly aren't feeling well and I think that it is best that you just leave this place immediately." She held her pruning shears tightly just in case the strange man made a move in her direction.

"He doesn't love you, Katherine. He doesn't deserve you. I have proof and I intend to use my knowledge and expose him." There was a wild look in the man's eyes.

"Peter, if that is truly who you are. It is quite obvious that you have something terribly wrong with you. I will not tell anyone about what we have just spoke about if you leave me at once." She was just about to call for her maid when the man excused himself.

"Please consider what I have told you. Good day, miss." Peter then turned around and walked at a brisk pace toward the stables.

Uncomfortable and bewildered with the handyman's odd statements, Katherine instructed that John, the stable boy, ready the coach for a trip into town. Within minutes, the coach was traveling to town at full speed. Katherine knew that it was forbidden for her to travel into town without her husband, but figured that since it was her husband that she was seeking that he would not be angry.

The coach pulled into town and parked near the large investment building where Matthew worked long hours each day. She had only been to this building once before but knew exactly where Matthew's office was located.

She brushed her skirts which were visibly soiled from when she was working in her rose garden, and attempted to appear calm. Escorted by John, she entered the building.

The secretary at the front desk instantly knew who she was but seemed nervous at her disheveled appearance. "Mrs. Wordly, what are you doing here?"

Katherine hesitated for a moment before speaking to the elderly secretary. "I...need to speak with my husband, immediately." Katherine could tell that all of the businessmen who were working at their desks had raised their heads to see what all of the commotion was about.

"I'm sorry, surely you know that your husband finishes work at precisely four o'clock every day. He would be home by now." The secretary peered over her spectacles toward Katherine, gazing at her oddly.

"Oh yes, I just thought that he might be working late tonight." Katherine suddenly aware of the strangeness of the situation, tried to appear as if she wasn't bothered by the fact that her husband wasn't at the office. "I suppose that maybe he stopped for a drink before returning home."

The secretary brightened. "Mr. Wordly never works late, my dear. He is a very social man. I'm sure that you might find him down at O'Donnels enjoying a pint. It's a gentlemen's club, but I'm sure that they will let John in."

"Thank you for your concern, excuse me." Katherine left the office and instructed John to take her to the mentioned club. Though he appeared reluctant, he did not question her request and complied.

As Katherine rode in the coach, she noticed that it was once again beginning to rain. She shivered as she watched out the window of the coach as it slowly traveled down the muddy main road. Desperate to have something else to concentrate on other than her absent husband's strange whereabouts, she became lost in the passing view of store windows and the glow of the lamps within. As they passed the grand windows of the hotel plaza restaurant, she instantly recognized someone from inside. Her heart sank as she stared at the handsome couple kissing within. It was her husband Matthew sitting with a pretty young girl whom she herself undoubtedly hadn't met before.

"Stop at once!" John pulled the horses to a stop in the middle of the road. Katherine didn't wait for John's help to exit the coach and ran across the muddy roadway to the window. The people inside seemed oblivious to the woman running toward the large window. Katherine stopped short of the entrance and stared inside, dumbfounded at the sight of her husband sitting, smiling and what appeared to be intimately speaking to this young lady. Part of Katherine wanted to run into the restaurant and question him, and the other part of her wanted to return home, excepting this moment as just one more negative thought to add to her already miserable life. Returning home was exactly what she would do.

Katherine boarded the coach and instructed John to take her home. She could tell by the expression on his face that he knew all about her husband's clandestine meetings with these other women. She wondered to herself about how many of them there were and exactly how long this had been going on.

Later that night when Matthew returned home, she didn't question him. She already knew that his answers would be tales that he had already prepared long before this day and didn't want to battle with him over the truth. His temper was far too much to compete with these days and at this point in their short marriage, she didn't care what he did. She just knew that she must find a way out of the hell that he custom made for her but she just needed to gather the strength to do just that.

Chapter Fifteen

IT WAS EARLY ONE morning when Katherine sneaked out of her and Matthew's sleeping quarters to tend to her topiaries. A few moments alone each morning was something that she direly needed to keep a hold of what was left of her sanity. The house's cold walls had become her dungeon and she unknowingly found herself to be just another piece of furnishing for her master Matthew to collect and adorn his household with. As she sat snipping quietly at the deadened fall foliage on her prize tea rose, she contemplated as to what mindless task she should conquer next in an attempt to pass the day away. She reached up and smoothed a wisp of unruly hair that had fallen into her view and suddenly sensed that someone was standing beside her.

Frightened, she instinctively gasped and raised her free arm to shield the blows that she expected. It was forbidden for her to be out in the gardens so early without so much as a maid to keep a watchful eye on her. She knew that if Matthew had found her there in the gardens alone, there would be hell to pay. When she did not receive the cruel punishment that she was all too familiar with, she turned and slowly stood, arm still raised, and faced the man the stood next to her. Finally able to raise her eyes, her heart quickened as she stared at the man before her.

It was not Matthew as she expected, but Ashton. "Put your arm down, child, it is I, Ashton. There is no need to ever fear me. I will not ever harm you as he surely has." Katherine gasped. She simply turned her face downward again and stared at her dirt-covered gloves, ashamed that he now knew of her cowering. She was embarrassed that she tolerated the abuse that Matthew put her through, and wanted desperately to forever keep the sick aspects of her marriage a secret, especially from Ashton.

Ashton reached down and placed his hand beneath her chin, lifting her face up so that her eyes met his. "Never sink before me. You are not beneath me. You mustn't let anyone make you feel less than who you really are. It was you who taught me that." Ashton sighed, wondering what became of the strong young lady that he once knew. The Katherine of the past would have gladly kicked a man in the shin for not announcing himself in her presence.

She stared at him as if he were a ghost, coming to haunt her for her misgivings. "This isn't real, you are gone. I am having illusions related to my despair, that is all." She blinked hard and stared back at him. The heavy English fog had surely created these visions. In the distance, she could hear a child crying. Concreting the idea that she had surely gone mad this time, she closed her eyes and allowed the vision to transpire more clearly in the fog. Ashton, still holding her hand, pulled her to her feet. Katherine was still unable to look the huge man square in the eye. She felt as if she ignored the specter, it would surely go away.

"Katherine, it's me. Pray God, woman, you must recognize

me?" He bent down on one knee to come into her view.

Her embarrassment flamed hotly in her cheeks though the morning was quite cold. Her eyes opened slightly to come upon the sight before her. "Ashton!" She didn't care at this point about her worry of hallucinations. She cared naught that she had gone mad, only that her dear Ashton was again holding her as he had so many months before in the past. His strong arms were wrapped around her body so tightly that she felt as though she would collapse. Their lips collided like the wind and the rain. The couple were soon lost in each other's embrace, completely oblivious to the world surrounding them. They held each other as their hands ravaged each other's bodies in immodest need as well as showing the love they clearly felt for each other.

Once again, Katherine heard a child coo softly in the distant fog. She pulled herself abruptly from Ashton's embrace. She smiled and laughed out loud for she knew now that this was surely a dream. She twirled around laughing, arms outstretched as Ashton danced with her silently. He rubbed his face in her hair and kissed her forehead like a madman. Happiness was once again gracing her heart. As she twirled around endlessly, still laughing, she abruptly heard a husky voice call to her from beyond the arbor. She stopped suddenly, arms quickly finding rest at her sides as she recognized her husband glaring at her.

His ill temper was evident, even through the dense fog and he stared at her as though she were a leper. "What on earth are you doing, woman? I have never seen such behavior. You are dancing as if the fairies are with you."

Katherine stared at him in contempt but was suddenly aware that she was indeed alone. She searched the hedges beside her for any sign of her lover, but could find nothing. The soft cries of a child in the forest had disappeared and she was once again alone. She peered to both sides of the path but could see no signs of Ashton's presence. The leaves were as they always were; the grass had not a blade disheveled. There were no footsteps in the frost as there would have been on the path, nor was there a wetness on her lips had her true love's vision been true. Looking at the seemingly untouched garden, she was certain that her sanity was lost.

Now silent, Katherine followed her husband to the house, still shaking with the excitement she had just experienced. She looked back at her fair roses and once again caught sight of her kind Ashton. His image was blurred in the fog, but she was sure that it was him, in one form or another, giving her strength to carry on for yet another day, permitting her a will to live despite her losses.

It was a few days later that Katherine was attending her embroidery when Matthew entered the room and came upon her humming softly to herself. "What is it this time, woman! Your music disturbs me. Not up to dancing alone in the gardens today?" Matthew's sarcasm did nothing to her. She was certain that she had gone mad and cared little of what Matthew thought of her now. Katherine's eyes shifted boldly toward her husband's. Smiling insanely, she continued to sing softly to herself, rocking gently in her chair. Matthew quickly found a reason to leave the room, clearly uneasy with his wife's strange behavior.

Chapter Sixteen

KATHERINE WAS DISGUSTED THAT she allowed herself, a Kenningston, to be treated so horribly by anyone these past few months, and vowed to herself one morning to take a hold of her life and change what she didn't like. The first step of changing her life would to find her dear Ashton. She decided to gather what information she could from her parents while having tea at the café after church one Sunday in hopes to discover the whereabouts of her dear Ashton.

"Mum, the night Ashton left, where did he say he was going?" Katherine didn't have much time and thought it was best to get straight to the point. Matthew had excused himself to finish up some work at the office and therefore Katherine seized the opportunity to question her family.

Mrs. Kenningston had instantly appeared to tense up as she searched for an appropriate answer. "Oh, Mr. Ashton? My dear, I believe he said that he was going to stay with some relatives in London, that is all of the information that he gave us before he left. Never mind about all that now, my dear. He is long gone, we must all move on." Her mother gave her that uneasy smile that she gave when she was uncomfortable with some aspect of the conversation.

"Yes, Mother, I understand, it's just that there are some things that I simply cannot lay to rest until I see him again." Katherine was once again beginning to feel unstable.

"Katherine, dear, you must forget about him. You have Matthew now." Mrs. Kenningston beckoned for the waiter to fetch her another cup of tea.

"Things aren't what they seem with myself and Matthew. I can't explain here or now, but you must believe me that it is imperative that I find Ashton. Please."

Mrs. Kenningston looked around her to make sure that there wasn't anyone listening to the details of their conversation. "You must understand, child, that if I tell you where he might be and you go seeking him, you must be prepared for what you will find. Things are not the same with him as you remember. There are things that we didn't tell you about."

"Mum, please." Katherine could feel her mother finally beginning to understand her desperation.

"What will you tell Matthew?" Mrs. Kenningston sipped her tea quietly.

"Nothing, I will just pack up the necessities and leave. Maybe I will tell him that I am going to visit Grandmother and will return in a few weeks. That will help ease him and not raise any suspicions." Katherine grasped her mother's hand. "I must do this, you understand."

"Yes, I know." Her mother looked to her daughter and knew that whatever was to become of this, it was the right thing to do.

Later that night when Matthew and Katherine were having their dinner, Katherine decided that it would be a good time to announce that she would be going away to London. "Mum told me that Grandmother isn't doing well. I would like to spend a few days with her if possible, just to give my last respects. I will leave in the morning." She nervously finished the last of her glass of wine.

Matthew gave her the familiar suspicious look that she was all too familiar with. "Your grandmother is ill?" He continued his stare at her knowing that she would falter if she was lying to him.

"Yes, Mum told me about it this morning after church. She said to talk to her if you need any information about where I will be staying." Katherine stared right back.

Matthew thought about her statements for a few moments and then replied, "I suppose that is acceptable, considering that it is your grandmother. But I will only let you go if you take Peter and John with you...for your protection, of course."

Before the break of dawn, Katherine and the two servants were on their way to the grand town of London. It was to be almost a day's drive to the outskirts of London so Katherine had taken along some items such as her embroidery and novels to keep her occupied. After many hours of traveling had passed, they had stopped along a riverbank to stretch their legs and to refresh themselves when Katherine decided to educate her escorts on the real reason that they were traveling to London. "Before we travel any further, I feel that I must inform you of the actual reason that we are going to London. I have misled you both regarding the details of our destination."

Before she could begin to explain, Peter interrupted. "There is no need to explain, Mrs. Wordly. We are both in suspect that you are ultimately in search of your former servant Mr. Ashton. We agree that you need to be as far away from Mr. Wordly as possible, before he hurts you any further. That is why John and myself accepted Mr. Wordly's request to escort you. We have no intentions of stopping you and feel that you are indeed in grave danger." Peter stared at his feet while he spoke.

"Mr. Wordly is not the man that you believe him to be. He had involved us in…dealings that we regret to have ever been a part of."

Katherine was uneasy with the two men's behaviors but pressed them for more information. "What do you two mean? What has he made the two of you do?"

"Never mind the details, miss. It is important that we move on now. Mr. Ashton will be able to protect you if he is the man that he is rumored to be." Peter motioned for Katherine to board the coach once more and they were off again on the long deserted road to London. She spent the next few hours contemplating what they had said. As they passed farmland littered with cattle, broken ruins of castles and battlements of long ago now deserted in the fog, she found relief instead of embarrassment that someone had offered to help her when she hadn't wanted to help herself. She didn't care of what criminal intentions they had been involved in alongside her husband, what mattered now is that she was leaving him, and she had their help.

They arrived in London before nightfall and stayed at a quaint inn on the outskirts of town. Katherine prepared herself for her search for Ashton, which they would attempt first thing in the morning. As the two servants bid her good night, she closed the door and found herself giddy with the excitement of seeing Ashton again shortly. She bathed and meticulously rolled her long hair. She hadn't fussed much with her appearance these last months since Matthew's affect had worsened. Any attention from him was unwanted and so she didn't want to entice his affections in anyway.

When morning came, she placed herself in one of her finest dresses. She knew that the London styles were often bold and she wanted to be able to fit in beautifully. When she exited the inn and boarded the coach, Peter couldn't resist remarking on her appearance.

"Mr. Ashton is a very lucky man to have the attentions of such a fine lady as you." He winked at her as she boarded the coach for what she had hoped was to be for the last time. She had the address that her mother had given to her for where Mr. Kenningston had been sending large sums of money each month. It was reportedly part of a generous severance agreement the Kenningstons offered Ashton when he decided to leave. Katherine decided to instruct the servants to go to this place first in hopes that Ashton would be home. It was, or at least appeared to be, the address of a stylish townhouse so Katherine imagined that it surely must be his current place of employment.

London was exactly as she had remembered. It had been many years since she had been to this great city but its magnificent structures held true to her memory. She was dearly impressed as she passed the grand hotels and businesses, noticing how all the townspeople seemed to be in such a hurry to be someplace or another, oblivious to her passing coach. She wondered to herself if her mild-mannered, quiet Ashton was happy in such a busy place as this. The excitement of seeing him again overwhelmed her immensely; she had much to tell her longtime friend. She just hoped that Matthew hadn't discovered that something was amiss in her story.

Peter announced that they were finally nearing the townhouse. Katherine could barely sit still and had to resist the urge to jump from the moving carriage and scream aloud Ashton's name. The fog had lifted and the high-class residential neighborhood was lit with bright sunlight peeking through the trees. As they pulled to the street that the townhouse was on, Katherine's eyes roved her streets for any signs of her past lover.

As the coach came to a stop, she saw nothing except for a quaint couple playing with their child in a close by park. Peter and John both escorted her from the coach and she took a deep

148

breath of the crisp town air. "Well, I guess we should try the house first. Mr. Ashton is rarely far from his work." She smiled but the two men could see that she was clearly nervous.

From the distance, Katherine could hear the child in the park giggling and she dreamed of how wonderful it would be if she and Ashton were to someday have a child of their own. As she gracefully climbed the steps of the townhouse she then heard what she thought was the familiar voice of Ashton. She hastily turned in the direction of the park and began to call out to him, now running in his direction.

Peter and John, though unsure of Katherine's intentions, followed her. "Mrs. Katherine, please slow down!"

As Katherine rounded the sidewalk now in full view of the park, she abruptly stopped and gasped.

"What is the matter, milady?" John immediately noticed the strange expression on Katherine's face.

Peter, also noticing the odd look on Katherine's face, spoke up. "Mrs. Katherine, did you injure yourself, possibly twist your ankle? Can we help you in any way?"

Katherine stood silent and motionless along the street side, unaware of anything that either of her servants were saying. Peter and John turned in the direction of her stare and realized at once the source of her turmoil. There, in the distance, was a baby stroller parked near a bench with a charming couple seated on it. It was unmistakably Ashton holding a small child, playing intently with it. Laughing and sitting beside him was Katherine's former young maid, Ann. Her worst fear had been realized. Ashton had fallen in love with someone else, and they now apparently had a child together. This was what all of the secrecy of his disappearance was all about. He obviously was too cowardly to tell her that he was in love with the young maid Ann.

Katherine whispered loudly to herself. "It can't be Ann. She couldn't possibly be anything but sixteen or seventeen now. She's just a child herself. What kind of sick ba…" Peter had pulled Katherine back in the direction of the coach, hoping not to attract any attention from Ashton and his new family.

Katherine seemed to be in some sort of shock as Peter tried to calm her. "Mrs. Katherine, I'm so sorry." He placed his hand on her chin and gently turned her away from the direction of the couple.

Tears streamed down Katherine's face as John helped her once again board the coach. "I'm sure that he loved you, Mrs. Katherine. He just couldn't possibly contend with the likes of Matthew, that's all. Surely you understand?" Katherine was speechless. She shakily boarded the coach and stared at the couple through the trees. Ashton and Ann? Was this what her mother meant about when she said that things are not the same as she had remembered?

Katherine heard Peter instruct John to take the reins, as he needed to speak with Mrs. Wordly. He entered the coach and spoke kindly to her. "Mrs. Katherine, is there anything that I can do for you? This is clearly upsetting to you and I am concerned."

"No, I'll be fine. Take me back to the inn immediately." Peter then instructed John to do so at Mrs. Wordly's request.

At the inn, Katherine excused herself and went directly to her room. It was a few hours after they had returned when she heard someone knock at her door. She found herself reluctant to answer. "Yes?" It was Peter. Although his appearance had frightened her so many months ago, she had found herself at ease with his presence, and in fact had found him to be quite likable and kind.

"I was wanting to speak with you… Privately." Peter lowered his voice so that he would not be heard by anyone but Katherine.

Katherine peered through the crack in the door and saw that John was not with him. "Yes, but just for a moment, I am feeling quite tired this eve and would prefer to be alone." She opened the door and the tall skinny handyman entered. After a moment of silence, she spoke again. "What is it, Peter?"

"I simply cannot allow you to go back to Mr. Wordly. I have been with him for many years and I know exactly what kind of person he really is. I will not go into details being that you are a lady, but for your safety, I cannot let you return. After some thought I have come to the realization that I am prepared and willing to care for you myself, if you'll have me."

Katherine was touched with the bold and unexpected kindness that she was receiving from one of her husband's servants, but knew that his proposal was never meant to be. "If you are referring to my husband's infidelity, I am ashamed to admit that I had prior knowledge of this. As for Matthew's temper, I too am frightened of my well-being, but I must return to him before it is too late, for all of us. Although I am flattered by your offer, I have since come to my senses. Mr. Ashton's unexpected change of heart has made me realize that I must return to Matthew and try to work things out. He is, after all, my husband and I must respect that. I don't know what I was thinking of after all."

Peter was clearly annoyed by her statements at appeared to take a moment to restrain himself. "I understand the importance of you respecting your promise to him, but I fear that if you return, he will ultimately kill you. I know that I am stepping beyond my bounds by speaking to you about this matter but surely you understand that I would not do so unless it was of grave importance."

"Peter, you must leave now. How dare you accuse my husband of such indecencies." She touched the locket around her neck. "I have no one now and so I simply must return to Matthew. I appreciate your sincerity, but I cannot include another life in my tribulations."

Peter left without saying another word and by the next afternoon, they were arriving at the house. Matthew hadn't even bothered to take the day off to greet her arrival though she

151

had sent word that she would be arriving early. As Katherine entered the house she felt the familiar cold chill that she had grown to expect when she was within its walls. Even Penne seemed colder than she had been but a few days before.

Later that night, Matthew returned home, smelling of sweet perfume and strong liquor. In an uncaring fashion, he asked about how Katherine's grandmother was feeling. "You returned sooner than I had expected, did your grandmother pass?"

Katherine noticed instantly that Matthew seemed bothered by her quick return. "No, I just wanted to be back here with you, that's all. I thought that it would please you." Katherine felt angered by his words. She sat at the chair just right of him at the table. "I know that I haven't always been the wife that you always dreamed of, but you could at least try to seem interested that I have returned."

Matthew stood up from his chair and addressed her harshly. "You will not speak to me in that tone while you live in my house!" He raised his hand to her but resisted the urge to strike her.

Katherine remained steadfast in her seat. "That's all right, dear Matthew. Go ahead and hit me. This is your house after all. Just remember that I am not one of your little whores that you must pay to love you." She smiled broadly at him. "You see, I don't love you. I suppose I never will. You can keep me in this beautiful house, give me nice things to wear, even choose my friends for me, but you will never have me...truly. Entitlement isn't everything; in fact, it means nothing to me at all at this point." Katherine began to feel the familiar ebb of insanity begin to sweep over her. She then rose and went to her reading room and began to write a letter to her former love Ashton stating that she needed to speak with him right away. She wanted to tell him that she had sought him out and how she felt about what she had found.

One week later Katherine received a letter stating that Ashton would be staying at the Kenningston's for two days on a social visit. He needed to speak to her and explain some things. Katherine thought that it was odd that he had wanted to speak to her at all. He was clearly happy with his new life.

That morning Katherine announced that she would be visiting her parents at the manor, directly after church.

Matthew looked up from his stacks of investment logs and eyed her carefully. "Just what makes you think that you deserve to go over there? Christ, Katherine, if I didn't know any better I would say that you are up to something. You are hardly home anymore."

"Mum wanted me over for tea, if I do not attend, she will think that I am ill and will come to see me here. But if that is what you prefer…." Katherine could feel a rush of nervousness in the pit of her stomach. Lying wasn't something that she was ever good at.

"Very well then, if you must go then so be it. I will expect you home in time for a late supper. Oh and, Katherine, my dear, if you are deceiving me in any way, I will have that precious horse of yours downed and fed to the hogs."

Katherine stormed out of the room in a fury, nearly knocking Penne to her knees. She ran to her room breathless with anger and dressed in an appropriate Sunday gown. While she messed with her hair, she mumbled to herself profanities that she had only heard her father speak when he could no longer control himself.

Peter helped Katherine board the coach and began their journey to the church. As usual, nearly every towns person had arrived for services, dressed in the best attire that their earnings could afford. Katherine seated herself in the pew next to her parents and glanced around for any sign of Ashton. The servants were usually seated at the back of the church but

Katherine saw no one that even resembled him.

After the hour of worship was over, Katherine followed her parents out to the awaiting coaches and began to board. As she climbed into her own, she gasped when she discovered that Matthew was seated inside waiting. "Matthew, what are you doing here?" Katherine tried not to sound disappointed.

"It has been awhile since I have had an encounter with your family at the manor, so I thought that I would join. Besides, the fresh air will do me some good."

He grasped her hand tightly and her heart sank. She knew that even if Ashton was at the manor waiting to speak with her, she would not be able to find a moment alone to speak with him. Even worse, if Matthew spied Ashton at the manor, he would surely suspect that it was a planned meeting. Katherine sat back and closed her eyes, dreading that she had ever chosen to go.

As the coaches pulled closer to the manor, Katherine's eyes roved the entranceway, expecting Ashton to walk out to greet her. She was sickened with the fear of her plan being discovered.

Even though frightened of what possibilities the next few hours beheld, she was somewhat comforted by the familiar grounds of the stately manor. Janice waited at the doorway to greet the oncoming coaches and escorted the inhabitants inside.

Katherine felt as if she was going to crawl out of her skin, both with the anticipation of seeing Ashton but also with the fear of Matthew realizing the importance of the visit. The familiar maids served the tea and gave no indication what so ever that there was another guest in the house. Katherine began to think that it was quite possible that Ashton hadn't come at all.

After nearly an hour, Katherine began to relax somewhat, feeling certain that if Ashton were indeed in the house, he would have presented himself by now. Katherine continued to fumble with the locket around her neck nervously in efforts to calm herself before Matthew had realized that something was causing her unease.

At last the tea was over and Matthew announced that he still had a lot of work to do before the week began and that they would be leaving. Katherine felt strangely relieved that the day's events would soon be over.

As they were once again seated in the coach, Katherine stared forlornly out of the window facing the pool area. Watching the now faded flowers pull further away, she found herself locking eyes with a man standing in her view. It was Ashton. She turned and placed her hands flat against the coach's single pained window as if they were going to somehow disappear and she might touch him. Ashton did not try to hide himself behind the giant oak tree that stood beside him, nor did he turn his face away so that he would not be discovered. He simply stood there as Katherine was driven away and mouthed the words 'I love you.'

Matthew suddenly realizing that Katherine was acting odd, jerked her away from the window. "What is the matter, dear girl, you looked as though you were about to fall out of the carriage?" He peered out the window that she was gazing through but saw nothing.

"Just a deer. That's all." Katherine sat back and contemplated the strangeness of the situation. Why hadn't Ashton come inside? What was he planning to speak to her about today?

Chapter Seventeen

YET ANOTHER CHRISTMAS HOLIDAY had arrived. Katherine's spirits were uplifted somewhat, but she was still not the happy woman that she was last holiday season. Katherine and Matthew were invited, as expected, to a gathering at the country club for Christmas Eve. The Kenningstons were to meet them there also. In fact, practically any person with any social status at all was invited to this formal gathering. It was the talk of the town and there would even be special guests and politicians arriving from as far as London to join in the festivities. Katherine was not up to parties these days. She had spent most of her winter days indoors; reading, sewing or whatever other simple-minded duties that she could think of to pass the time. She felt as if she were a flower withering in the darkness.

The weather had grown cold, as it had always done this time of the year, and Matthew was beginning to find more and more reasons for Katherine not to venture into town. Matthew decided that it would be best for her to have the tailors come to the house to have her fitted for a new dress; he was determined to have his new bride be the object of his comrades' jealous attention. The party was tomorrow night and they would have to prepare accordingly. Matthew was never afraid to show evidence of his money or financial status. In fact, he loved to have nothing but the finest things, just so others could gloat over them. Though he enjoyed fanciful things, he enjoyed even more making others feel inferior, especially Katherine.

It was the day of the holiday festivities and Katherine once again was a spectacular sight. The angelic woman showed no signs whatsoever of the tragedies that she had survived this past year. Penne was fussing over the lady of the house's hair as Matthew walked in to her dressing quarters, unannounced as usual. "Katherine, my love, you look wonderful." His eyes roved over the entire length of her new dress, slowing with each delicate curve of her body. His eyes focused on the locket around her neck. "Why do you insist on always wearing that atrocious-looking locket?"

Katherine, though mortally insulted, could see that his temper was instantly rising once again. She tried to distract the attention from herself by dropping her hairbrush on the floor by her feet. "Oh dear, how did I ever become so clumsy...."

Still Matthew persisted, staring wildly at the locket around her neck. "Don't you ever take that retched thing off? Where did you get it anyway?" Matthew took a step closer to her to inspect it. He touched it with his forefinger and sneered at her. "It is positively despicable. I dare not think that it is real gold?" Matthew stumbled somewhat to the side, indicating that he had started the celebration early.

Katherine tried to turn away, but he caught her firmly around the shoulders. She winced in pain as his fingers dug sharply into her skin. He then, in one fluid motion, reached up and tore the locket from her neck. Katherine screamed aloud as

157

all of the happy memories flooded from her mind. The only remembrance of her child and Ashton was gone, ripped from her just like her childhood.

Taking a deep breath, she concentrated on collecting her thoughts. From somewhere within herself, she vowed that she would not cry this time. There was nothing left of her pride and she didn't care what he did to her anymore. Daringly she lifted her head and looked him deep into the eyes.

"Matthew, you may not believe the words that I speak to you now, but someday, somewhere, you will pay for the things that you have done to me." Leaving Matthew stunned and in silence, she turned and walked past him straight out of the room. Penne gathered the gifts for their friends and family and followed Katherine to the waiting coach.

Matthew was not far behind and boarded the coach fuming mad. "You will not ever address me in that manner again!" Matthew thought that Katherine was just keenly interested in what he had to say because she spoke not another word to him on the way to the club. He spent the entire time on the way to the party scolding her for threatening him.

Katherine simply smiled to herself and nodded at him as if answering some secret question that only she knew the answer to.

The club was once again bright with stateliness. The guests were just beginning to arrive and there were carolers at the door to greet them. A large tree was lit up with miniature candles and the room was filled with a glorious pine and cinnamon scent. The tables were adorned with soft glowing lamps, illuminating the trays of festive dishes. Matthew promptly seated Katherine at her family's table and then excused himself to the bar to have a few drinks with his father and some of his colleagues.

Katherine faced her mother and gave what was to be her best performance ever. She smiled sweetly and then spoke carefully. "You look beautiful, Mum. How have things been with you this week?" Katherine laboriously tried to have as normal as possible of a conversation with her parents, trying to cover up the fact that Matthew had been so cruel to her just hours before, but was having difficulties trying to find things to talk about.

"Katherine, my dear, are you not feeling well? You seem so quiet this eve." Mrs. Kenningston noticed that Katherine's thoughts seemed to be someplace else.

Katherine smiled and her hand instinctively reached for the locket around her neck, but it was not there. She glared across the room at Matthew. "Oh, just not in the mood for festivities, that's all." She smiled a broad, false smile. The waiters were gracefully beginning to serve the roasted duck and champagne.

"So, my dear, how have things been at the house? Are you and Matthew enjoying yourselves?" questioned Mrs. Kenningston, appearing to sense that there was something amiss about the young couple.

Katherine knew that this type of innocent conversation was just her mother's way of prying into her life. "Actually, Mother, I am quite miserable, and secretly wish that I would die in my sleep." She momentarily gave her mother an emotionless glare.

"Bravo, dear, you always had that dark humor about you. Your wit still astounds me." Her mother gave a hearty laugh.

Katherine smiled at the way her mother found her statement funny and changed the subject. "Where is father?" Mr. Kenningston was no longer seated at the table, and neither had heard him excuse himself.

"I don't know? He was sitting here a moment ago." Something in the tone of her mother's voice made Katherine think that her mother was hiding something. She could see Matthew across the hall engaged in deep conversation with a beautiful young lady from her church. Katherine was all too familiar with her husband's attentions being elsewhere nor did

159

she care to compete for it this night.

After dinner, Katherine stood near the grand hall's tree. As she stared at the lights, it made her think of Ashton. She wondered where he was at that moment, if he was happy. She had long gotten over the anger of him leaving her and now all that remained were questions and fond memories. Although she was still wondering what the strange correspondence from months ago meant, she had now dismissed its relevance. Maybe she had dreamed the whole thing, maybe not, it didn't matter to her anymore. She stared at the mass of people who had begun to dance to the orchestra. She found herself feeling happy for those enjoying themselves. It was, after all, supposed to be a happy time of year.

As she was humming to the music and fiddling with her gloves as she always did when consumed by thought, she caught sight of a dissimilar face walking into the hall with her father. Trying not to draw attention to herself, she nonchalantly gazed in their direction, curious as to who would have the audacity to show up to the party this late in the evening. From the way the man was clothed, he was just another wealthy politician acquaintance of her father's, though she was unsure from this distance. Still she felt intrigued by the stranger and stared across the room, blinking her eyes into focus. Slowly, she walked into the crowd of dancers to get a better view when a peculiarly frantic sensation came over her.

It instantly seemed as though the room was bizarrely silenced and the dancers twirled and bowed noiselessly. The tall man at the doorway seemed to be looking for someone as his eyes roved over the crowd intensely. Her father seemed to be helping the man locate someone in the crowd. Katherine, halfway across the dance floor by this time, slowed to a stop as she just stared confusedly at the man some distance before her, dressed in the expensive formal suit. Some of the dancers were now stopping to see what she was looking at so alarmingly.

The finely dressed man had noticed her from across the

room and seemed to recognize her. Steadily, he began to gracefully approach her through the onlooking crowd. She felt as if she couldn't breathe or move, possibly in another one of her fantasies. Her feet were heavy as stones and her heart leapt at the spectacle before her.

"Ashton?" She tried to cry out but her voice was merely a harsh whisper, the people nearest to her stopping to see whom she was calling to.

Spotting her again, the man was soon working his way through the crowd as the dancers parted to give him way. Even the orchestra seemed to notice the commotion and slowed their pace. Ashton had soon woven his way through the dancers and now stood directly in front of the stunned Katherine. Her mouth was moving but she could no longer find the strength to say words.

Glad that he had finally found Katherine, Ashton paused, standing inches before her just looking at the angel standing before him. First touching her cheek as if it were made of glass, he then passionately took her into his arms and kissed her deeply, for everyone to see. He was not ashamed this time to show his true love for this woman before him.

Katherine, forgetting who and what she was this time, kissed him back…equally. "I have always loved you, and only you." There was an explosion of whispers and voices throughout the room.

Matthew, finishing his drink at the bar, saw that there was something happening on the other side of the ballroom floor. Curiosity got the better of him and he rose, setting his glass on the hard wood, and approached the crowd of whispering people. He was alarmed when he saw the Kenningstons speaking to someone in the center of the commotion. The voices surrounding him seemed to be saying something about—Katherine?

Hurriedly shoving people out of his way, Matthew

approached the center of the uproar. He was soon eye to eye with Mr. Kenningston who was standing beside his wife and a strangely familiar man. He stared in disbelief as he realized that this tall man was their former servant, Ashton, and he was kissing his wife!

"Katherine, you step away from him this instant!" Matthew demanded, sounding more like a whining child than a grown man. Ashton towered over Matthew and fiercely stared down at him. He recognized at once that this was the man that loved his wife, and that he had always known she never stopped loving back.

Ashton's voice echoed in the silent room. "Good evening, Mr. Wordly. It appears that you need now to say your goodbyes to the Lady Katherine as I have come to claim which was never yours to begin with." Katherine remained close to Ashton, abruptly realizing the intensity of the moment.

Matthew, not believing his own ears, said, "Excuse me? Sir, I believe that you must be mad!" The crowd surrounding them hushed.

Mr. Kenningston spoke up. "After many months of investigation, and some unlikely assistance from some of your personal staff, Mr. Ashton has discovered what kind of person you really are. We know everything that you have done, not just the things that you mercilessly put my daughter through. We have notified the authorities and they will be here from London momentarily."

Matthew look astonished. "I-I don't know what you are eluding to, I assure you all that this is nonsense." The music had still not resumed playing and all eyes were on the two men.

Clearing his throat, Mr. Kenningston continued, "We have proof that you have been the one behind the attacks on the local women and Mr. Ashton last year." Mr. Kenningston took a step towards Matthew. There were gasps throughout the crowd. In a hushed tone he finished. "I am going to make you pay for every ounce of pain that you put my dear Katie through, you ungodly bastard."

Ashton interrupted angrily. "You are a very sick man who has gone to any and all means to get what you wanted. This is to be the end of it all." He glanced downward and gave Katherine a sorrowful look.

Matthew charged towards Ashton. "You have no proof! How dare you make such accusations! I shall have you jailed for this!" The anger clearly overwhelming Matthew as he took a step toward his wife. Katherine began to feel herself shrink familiarly as he forcefully jerked her away from Ashton. "Come now, Katherine, let's leave this place. I do not associate with...servants." Katherine took a step backward away from Matthew and stood steadfast near Ashton.

Everything now began to make heartbreaking sense to Katherine. The odd statements that Matthew had made on occasion, his strange association with the man who looked strikingly like Timothy Barnes, his late nights out 'working.' From somewhere deep inside, Katherine found the strength and courage within her to speak. She took a few steps forward and staring Matthew deep into the eyes, she said, "I will not leave this place with you, not now, and not ever again." She defiantly lifted her chin and stood tall. "I believe you have something that belongs to me in your breast pocket." Ashton and Mr. Kenningston stared at each other questioningly.

Matthew smiled cunningly and reached into his pocket removing the locket. The lights of the room reflected sharply off the polished gold. He then held it out high for Katherine to grasp, but now possessed a bizarrely crazed look upon his face.

As Katherine approached and boldly reached upward for the necklace, Matthew slapped her hard across the face with his free hand and for a moment the room went black. "Whore." Katherine was knocked completely off her feet and fell backward into Mr. Kenningston who had barely caught her.

Ashton unflinchingly lunged forward and punched Matthew squarely in the face. Matthew stumbled, then gained his balance and glared at Ashton, splatters of red now scattered over his cheek. "You still have proven nothing." He wiped the flow of blood from his nose. A look of disgust came over Matthew as Ashton was attentively looking Katherine over and he spat at her, narrowly missing them both.

"If it is proof that you need, then I will graciously comply." Ashton then turned and faced the entranceway to the hall where he beckoned for Katherine's former maid who was standing quietly in the shadows. "Ann!" Ashton calmly called for the servant girl.

Shyly, Ann sifted through the crowd until she was standing beside Ashton. Again whispers broke out across the sea of people. Katherine was quick to notice that she had an odd bundle in her arms that appeared to be her child wrapped in a thick shawl. Her heart saddened as she remembered seeing Ashton sitting with her on the bench in the London Park.

"Ann, is this not the man who beat and ravaged you nearly to death over a year ago?" Ashton spoke gently to the maid.

"Yes, sir," she answered in a quivering voice and at once gave Katherine an embarrassed look. There were excited voices and questioning looks throughout the room.

Matthew looked repulsed by the young maid's accusations. "You will not take a servant's word over a Wordly's. You surely have paid that girl to speak!"

Mr. Kenningston stepped directly in front of Matthew. It was at that time that Matthew's father broke through the crowd and stood by Mr. Kenningston. "Even if that were true, you have treated my daughter with the utmost disrespect. I am ashamed that I ever gave you my blessing." Mr. Kenningston turned as his wife appeared slowly behind him.

Mrs. Kenningston had tears streaming down her face and looked pleadingly at Katherine. "Katherine, we have made a grave mistake and I only hope that you will be able to forgive us. We have done what we could to help Mr. Ashton in his quest to find your attackers, in hopes that someday you will find it within yourself to forgive us." Mrs. Kenningston looked sadly at Ann and then to her daughter.

Ashton reached out and removed the shawl from the baby that Ann was holding and gently grabbed a hold of the child, comfortably lifting her up to his shoulder. "Katherine, I have the proof that everybody is waiting for. I would like to present to you my dearest Julianne."

Katherine utterly stunned, held her hands to her face as she cried silently, unable to believe what had transpired before her. Katherine's child, now nearly eight months old, was the identical image of herself and Matthew Wordly. The striking blue eyes and small birthmark on the cheek was all that Katherine needed to see that Ashton was right. She realized then that she had been terribly mistaken about Ashton and Ann's relationship. The child was not a product of Ashton and Ann's fictitious relationship, but was of her own.

"Mr. Kenningston was kind enough to send Ann with me to assist in caring for the child as I attended my studies in London." Ashton placed the child in its mother's arms where she rightfully belonged. She had not paid any mind to the odd birthmark before in the few precious hours that she initially shared with her baby girl, but now had no doubt that this child was the very child that she bore from her rapist.

"Ashton, thank you." She was speechless. She stared at the child and sweet Julianne stared back almost knowingly, cooing softly to her mother. Katherine sank to the floor and cried out loud, she had what she had always wanted. Ashton and Julianne were now not only a figment of her distraught imagination.

Katherine turned to her husband and faced him for one last time. "How could you do this to me? How could you carry on this charade that we have called our lives and not show an ounce of remorse toward me, I am your wife!"

Matthew cruelly looked at her and then to their child. Her eye was beginning to swell where he had hit her and he smiled coolly. "My dear Katherine, you were my whore long before our wedding day. Don't act as if you didn't ask for this." He turned, bid his father good night, and left the club.

The London authorities were waiting for Matthew when he left the ballroom. He was trying to leave quietly to avoid prosecution but it was now time for him to pay for the terrors that he had done to these women. He was a rapist, a liar, and a fraud. He only wanted Katherine for a prize. He had been stalking her while she had lived at the Kenningston mansion for years, waiting for an opportunity to move. He planned an elaborate scheme to attack Katherine and the others, making it look as though it was a coup of lower-class radicals trying to make a statement. Timothy Barnes, now known to Katherine as Peter Stone, had fallen in love with Katherine and found it within his heart to turn himself in after seeking out Ashton and confessing everything. This would ultimately prove to be the information that Ashton had been seeking for months.

It would be later discovered that Matthew wanted Katherine's family's money and he wanted her. Now, because of his greed, he will have neither. Ashton had proven and explained everything to Mr. Wordly about his son's misgivings. Now Matthew's own father would not save him and Katherine was free at last.

Chapter Eighteen

IT HAD BEEN MONTHS since Matthew had gone to prison. Katherine had to appear before the court magistrate and explain, in horrific detail, each terrible event that led up to this. She was able to, with Ashton's help, put the past behind her. With time, she was even able to forgive her parents for the terrible lies that they had placed upon their only child.

After having her marriage to Matthew dissolved due to fault, abuse and infidelity, Katherine was able to marry her first and only love. Ashton and Katherine were married in a small ceremony at their townhouse in London, though the baby, Julianne, was clearly the center of entertainment. The couple stood before their friends and family and announced their love for each other. It would be in less than a year that Katherine would happily bear another child, this time a son.

"Ashton, look! Julianne is walking!" Katherine held her arms out to their daughter. Once again her belly was expanding far beyond the limits that her normal dresses would allow, so she sat comfortably on the floor in her plush robe. Ashton peered over his textbooks and drawings, beaming. There was a warm glow about the London townhouse.

"She is beautiful, just like her mother." Katherine blushed. Ashton had always made her feel wonderful. Ashton rose and gathered his books and supplies. "I'm off to my presentation at the university. Wish me luck!"

When Ashton left the manor with Julianne, Mr. Kenningston paid Ashton generously. He had been attending the London University since, now only a few short months from being a licensed physician. Ann had traveled with Ashton, compliments of Mr. Kenningston, to care for the child while Ashton spent his days studying with England's finest scholars. His love for Katherine had encouraged him to pursue his dreams, and now he had Katherine as his wife, and claimed Julianne as his own. Though Ashton was not a lord of an estate, or a top politician, he was the man that she loved. With this love, she didn't care that at that moment she was…presently untitled.

Printed in the United States
31958LVS00001B/103